"I Sense There's A Whole Lot More To Scarlet Anders And I Want The Chance To Get To Know Every Bit Of Her."

As his gaze roamed her face, her throat, a dangerous fizzy feeling sailed through her body, calling her, drawing her, and as if tugged by an invisible string, she tipped a fraction closer, too. Then one corner of his mouth curved up and, appalled by her behavior—at her craving—she jerked back again.

"Don't look at me like that. You're too…" She emptied her lungs, took another shallow breath. "You're too close."

"It's going to be difficult," he said. "Sitting beside you all night. Telling myself that I shouldn't."

"Shouldn't what?"

In that deep drugging voice, he murmured, "Kiss you, of course."

Dear Reader,

What more exciting place for a Harlequin Desire series to be set than Washington, D.C.! So much glamour. So many secrets. Always so much at stake.

In *A Wedding She'll Never Forget,* Ariella Winthrop continues to unravel the big questions surrounding her past and links to the incoming president, and investigations are underway to unmask the culprits responsible for those far-reaching White House leaks. In the meantime, work at D.C. Affairs—the district's premiere party-planning company—must go on.

Ex White House PR specialist Caroline Cranshaw is getting married, and the heroine of this book—socialite and D.C. Affairs's co-proprietor Scarlet Anders— intends to make her friend's wedding everything Caroline has imagined. Only, Scarlet finds her usually pristine feathers being ruffled by the incredibly persistent, uncommonly sexy best man. Australian technology billionaire Daniel McNeal is Scarlet's polar opposite and seems intent on stirring up all kinds of trouble for her with an annoying amount of ease. She'd sooner forget that man…if only she could.

When Scarlet's wish comes true, it's Daniel who suddenly finds he has trouble on his hands. And more than seduction on his mind.

Each story in this *Daughters of Power* collection is steeped in intrigue, scandal and, best of all, riveting romance. I hope you enjoy Scarlet and Daniel's installment!

Best wishes,

Robyn

Keep up to date with Robyn's latest releases and news at www.robyngrady.com.

ROBYN GRADY

A WEDDING SHE'LL NEVER FORGET

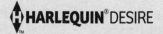

Special thanks and acknowledgment to Robyn Grady
for her contribution to the
Daughters of Power: The Capital miniseries.

Recycling programs
for this product may
not exist in your area.

ISBN-13: 978-0-373-73229-6

A WEDDING SHE'LL NEVER FORGET

Printed in U.S.A.

Books by Robyn Grady

Harlequin Desire

The Billionaire's Bedside Manner #2093
Millionaire Playboy, Maverick Heiress #2114
Strictly Temporary #2169
*Losing Control #2189
A Wedding She'll Never Forget #2216

Silhouette Desire

The Magnate's Marriage Demand #1842
For Blackmail...or Pleasure #1860
Baby Bequest #1908
Bedded by Blackmail #1950
The Billionaire's Fake Engagement #1968
Bargaining for Baby #2015
Amnesiac Ex, Unforgettable Vows #2063

*The Hunter Pact

Other titles by this author available in ebook format.

ROBYN GRADY

was first published with Harlequin Books in 2007. Her books have since featured regularly on bestseller lists and at award ceremonies, including a National Readers' Choice Award, a Booksellers' Best Award, CataRomance Reviewers' Choice Award and Australia's prestigious Romantic Book of the Year Award.

Robyn lives on Queensland's beautiful Sunshine Coast with her real-life hero husband and three daughters. When she can be dragged away from tapping out her next story, Robyn visits the theater, the beach and the mall (a lot!). To keep fit, she jogs (and shops) and dances with her youngest to Hannah Montana.

Robyn believes writing romance is the best job on the planet and she loves to hear from her readers. So drop by www.robyngrady.com and pass on your thoughts!

With thanks to my fellow *Daughters of Power* authors—
Barbara Dunlop, Michelle Celmer, Rachel Bailey,
Andrea Laurence and Jennifer Lewis.
Wonderful to work with you all!

And a special shout-out for our brilliant series editor,
Charles Griemsman. Always a pleasure.

* * *

Daughters of Power: The Capital
*In a town filled with high-stakes players,
it's these women who really rule.*

Don't miss any of the books
in this scandalous new continuity
from Harlequin Desire!

One

Angels live among us.

This one was balanced on a stepladder, decorating an arch strewn with sunflowers and sparkling cupids. Her chic up-sweep of red-gold hair drew attention to the emeralds sparkling on each earlobe, jewels that paid homage to the color of her eyes. Together with a dark skirt and peach silk blouse, the package said *refined* as well as *hold-me-back sexy.*

A pair of black pumps were paired neatly at the ladder's feet, and as she stretched to hang the final garland, one black-stockinged leg stretched out, too. Crossing his arms, Daniel McNeal butted a shoulder against the doorjamb and came to a conclusion. He'd bet all he was worth—and that was a lot—that one kiss from this angel could bring a mere mortal to his knees.

Spending time with a Washington wedding planner usually didn't feature on his to-do list. The only reason Daniel was here now was to tend to his best mate's upcoming nuptials.

But frankly, right this minute he couldn't think of a single place he'd rather be.

Although, at a distance, she faced him, she hadn't noticed him yet. As she finished hanging the final cupid and began her descent, he pushed off the doorjamb and, looking forward to the introduction, sauntered over. A heartbeat later, her footing somehow slipped. Gravity pulled her weight backward and, with a delicate yip, she lost her grip. As both arms swept over her head, Daniel sprinted. Lunged. Thankfully he caught her before she hit the ground.

Heart pumping, he straightened while his angel's wide green eyes stared up at the ceiling and her chest heaved with fright. She sucked back a fortifying breath. Eventually her startled gaze found his.

"I've been up that ladder dozens of times," she said. "I've never slipped." The bows of her lips trembled on a grateful smile. "I really need to thank you."

"I know the ideal way. Have dinner with me tonight."

She coughed out a laugh. Then she blinked, frowned and looked at him hard. "I don't even know your name."

"Daniel McNeal."

Recognition lit her face. "Daniel McNeal of Waves fame. The social networking site. I recognize the face now. You're Australian, yes?"

He nodded. "And you must be Scarlet Anders."

She was a partner here at DC Affairs with Ariella Winthrop—the woman who'd recently been labeled as the incoming president's secret love child. The claim, made by an American News Service reporter in a toast at an inauguration gala, had set the nation back flat on its behind. The obvious question was: If Ariella was indeed President Morrow's daughter, who was responsible for the leak? And just how deep did that fissure go?

Scarlet Anders was still gazing up at him. "So you're here about a wedding, Mr. McNeal?"

"Yes." He lifted her a fraction higher. "But not my own."

As if she were pleased to hear it, her perfect smile spread. But then her eyes rounded again and she wriggled until he had no choice but to set her down on her two stockinged feet. After patting back an errant curl flopped over one eye, she straightened her skirt, slipped on her shoes.

"Much better." Exhaling, she squared her shoulders and folded her hands loosely before her. "Now we can talk business."

"I was fine talking the other way." *While I held you in my arms.*

Her cheeks flushed a flattering shade of pink before she schooled her features and got the conversation back on track.

"So you're here regarding a wedding?"

"I'm Max Grayson's best man."

Like a kid who'd found her Christmas gifts early, she tipped up on her toes and pressed her hands against her drop pearl necklace in excitement. If not for etiquette, she might have thrown out her arms and hugged him.

"Max is engaged to one of my closest friends, Caroline Cranshaw," she said. "Every occasion DC Affairs takes on is special but we want Cara's day to be beyond brilliant."

"My goal exactly."

"In that case, I'm doubly pleased to meet you, Mr. McNeal."

When she extended her hand, he fought the urge to lift her fingers and brush his lips over the smooth underside of her wrist. Instead, he smiled, shook and ever so gently squeezed.

"Call me Daniel," he said. "We're all friends here, right?"

"Friends." She blinked. "Yes, of course."

When Scarlet tugged her hand away, her palm came to rest high on her stomach before she crossed to a display table set up in this room, one of three used to present wedding ceremony themes and displays.

"I was mulling over Cara's color scheme this morning." Her French-tipped nails traced over satin samples until she stopped at one. He couldn't help but notice. Third finger, left hand, no bling.

"Pastel pink is so pretty for a bride," she said, and he chuckled.

"Unfortunately, not so hot for us guys."

She flicked him a questioning glance before going on.

"Cara put a few suggestions forward. We'll work together over the coming weeks to make sure both she and Max are happy." She turned to him, holding the pink swatch she liked between them. "I appreciate you dropping in to introduce yourself. We'll speak again at the rehearsal dinner, I'm sure."

"Sounds official."

"It's meant to be fun. Relaxed."

A grin eased across his face. "Fun and relaxed work for me."

When he didn't move but rather continued smiling into those entrancing spring-green eyes, she held her stomach again and asked, "Did a specific query or concern bring you here today?"

Needing to concentrate on matters other than whether Scarlet Anders drank coffee or juice with breakfast—whether she wore lace or her birthday suit to bed—he drew back, tugged an ear.

"Max and I have been good friends for many years," he said. "We know everything there is to know about each other. Frankly, when I heard the news, I was surprised. It's not every day a guy's closest mate lets the world know he's found the girl of his dreams. Given what he'd told me in the past, I'd never imagined him married. Unless you count a man being married to his work."

She gave a faint shrug. "Priorities change."

"Seems so. After meeting Cara, seeing them together, I'm nothing but pleased for them both—for the wedding as well as the baby on the way. He's a lucky man to have found that kind of happiness."

Her guarded expression softened as she lowered the swatch of material to her side. Then she caught herself and, a little embarrassed, smiled again.

"I didn't take you for a romantic."

He cocked a brow. *A romantic?* He was merely making a point.

"Thing is," he went on, "there's nothing I wouldn't do to support them on their day and beyond."

"That's exactly how I feel."

"I'd hoped you'd say that, because I need your help. I'd like to inject a little fun into the whole shebang."

"Such as?"

"I'm thinking some good ol' Aussie humor."

One eyebrow slowly arched. "Aussie…humor?"

"Nothing outrageous."

Her lips twitched. "No kangaroos in bow ties, then?"

"Actually, I'd thought of flying in a couple of crocs from Kakadu." Her face slipped before she realized he was kidding. Given that bland look, Scarlet Anders, however, was not amused.

"I've had the privilege of being best man for a few of my mates," he explained. "I like to do something special on the day. It's become a bit of a tradition."

"Put a list together." She laid the fabric sample down and gazed at it, straightening it twice. "I'll give you our contact details and I'll see what we can do. As long as what you have planned doesn't interrupt protocol or good taste, of course."

His jaw shifted. Apparently this angel also came with a good dollop of diva thrown in.

"I didn't want to interrupt anything so much as add to it," he pointed out.

"In the outback I'm sure things are far more...impromptu."

"I don't live in the outback. Never have."

"Perhaps you should." Giving him a once-over—jeans, loafers, casual button-down, cuffs folded back—she tempered her dry tone with a backhanded compliment. "I mean, you're obviously the rugged type."

"Now that depends on your definition of rugged."

When his gaze penetrated hers, challenging Scarlet to look more deeply, too, she emitted a barely audible noise; she was agitated but also intrigued. Then her shoulders squared again and she headed for the door with the kind of gliding air only the refined and privileged could pull off.

"I hate to be rude," she said, "but I'm on a tight schedule this afternoon."

"Which brings us back to my earlier suggestion. We can talk more about my ideas over dinner."

"Given the circumstances—" her pert nose wrinkled "—inappropriate, I'm afraid."

His grin was wry. "I'm the guy who saved your life, remember? The thought of sharing time with me over a three-course meal can't be that bad."

"On the contrary—" She cut herself off. Then, cheeks pink again, she nodded cordially. Purposefully. "It was good to have met you."

Right then he should have walked—tipped his head, said goodbye and put this whole "helping with the wedding" business behind him. Except, from the moment he'd laid eyes on her, he'd been fascinated. Inexplicably, totally charmed. No getting away from the fact. His mind was made up.

His pursuit of Scarlet Anders had only begun.

* * *

When Daniel McNeal closed the distance separating them—that confident, lazy gaze fused with hers—every one of Scarlet's senses flared up to a brilliant blue heat and the joints in her knees seemed to melt. Then her stomach muscles knotted twice over and her heartbeat throbbed through her blood so deeply she became dizzy.

This can't be. We've only just met—and he's going to kiss me?

With everything happening in agonizing slow motion, she had more than enough time to stop him—stop *herself*— from leaning in, letting her eyes drift shut and, for some wild half-witted reason, make the biggest mistake of her life. She needed to remember that other man, the history they'd built and the stable future they seemed destined to share.

In her mind's eye, snapshots of her parents' faces blinked up—smiling, approving, toasting her future happiness. If they could read her mind now—could know how her body was responding—her mother and father would probably disown her. Not that Scarlet wasn't shocked enough for all three of them. She hadn't been brought up to behave like this.

Clenching her hands, Scarlet broke her gaze from his, took a shaky step back and noticed another person in the room. With her mouth agape, the florist from next door was staring at Scarlet as if the usually restrained party planner had transformed into a tassel-twirling tramp.

"Katie." Willing away the heat lighting her cheeks, Scarlet wound an ornery curl back off her burning face. "What are you doing here?"

While Daniel McNeal straightened and slotted his hands in the back pockets of his jeans, five-foot-two Katie, in her trademark orange bib-apron, edged forward.

"No one's on reception," Katie replied. "I came right through. Sorry. Didn't realize you had company."

As usual, manners kicked in. Scarlet rolled an introductory hand toward her bold but sexy guest.

"Katie Parker, meet Daniel McNeal."

Katie said, "Pleased to meet you," while her curious gaze raked his frame. "You look incredibly familiar," she said. "And that name…"

Scarlet groaned to herself. No need to get into a big conversation about this man's celebrity status, Waves or how every person in the galaxy was a member of that social media site, including herself. She only wanted her unsettling visitor gone. Needed to get her buzzing head back in the game.

With a disciplined gesture, she indicated the door. "Mr. McNeal was just leaving."

"That I was. We'll talk soon," he advised Scarlet before turning to Katie and saying, "Try to convince her to have dinner with me, will you?"

With a wink, he strolled out the door. Scarlet thought she heard him whistling while Katie shook her blond mane and rubbed her brow.

"I'm confused," Katie said. "He asked you on a date?"

"He was joking."

"He was dead serious. Which is fantastic because, let's face it, that guy is grade-A gorgeous. And charming. And melt-your-bones sexy—"

Rolling her eyes, Scarlet moved off. "Katie, please."

"Believe me, that guy is into you. And, if you don't mind me saying, it looks like the feeling is mutual. If I hadn't walked in, I bet you'd be kissing him now."

"No, I would not." Rearranging flowers near the base of the arch, she mumbled an admission. "I'd already decided against it."

"I *knew* it!"

Restless, Scarlet moved to the stepladder. "You also know

I'm in a relationship with a man any woman would be proud to call her own."

"Truthfully, Scarlet? From what I've seen, Everett Matheson III doesn't light any of my fires."

"Everett and I are well suited. He's predictable. Upstanding. Well-educated—"

"You forgot boring," Katie muttered.

"He has a strong work ethic. He'll make a responsible husband and father."

"But are you in love? Do you shiver with longing every time you think of him?"

Scarlet's stomach muscles kicked. She didn't float around on a cushion of clouds for *any* reason, including a man. Filling her lungs, she lifted the stepladder and let the legs snap shut.

"I was brought up to respect myself, which means not falling head over silly heels with the first charmer who throws a line my way." Scarlet took her ladder and headed for the storage closet to put it away. "I'm not that kind and you know it."

Sticking both hands in her apron's front pocket, Katie sighed like it was the end of the world. "After Cara and Max's big announcement, bet Everett will ask you soon, too."

"He already has. Last night." She set the ladder down in the storage closet and shut the door. "He hired a horse-drawn carriage. French champagne and crystal flutes were waiting in an ice bucket on the seat. After he proposed, he went through all the reasons we made such a good match. The ring's a family heirloom. It did hang on my finger a little. We need to have it resized."

The eight-carat hand-cut ruby set in a circle of diamonds made an exquisite engagement ring. She hated to think of the insurance he'd need to even take it out of the safety deposit box. When he'd mentioned having a replica made for everyday use, she'd laughed. Everett had a sharp wit sometimes.

Katie mumbled, "I should say congratulations—"

"Thank you."

"—but I'll also say you don't have to go through with it. No invitations have been sent. No venues booked…"

"You're a good friend—" Scarlet walked past the florist and her pleading gaze "—but I really don't need this."

At the samples table, Scarlet got busy laying violet, cream and royal-blue swatches in an arc while Katie made half an effort to change the subject.

"Who was that Adonis, anyway?" she asked. "I know the face. Is he some new whiz kid on the political scene?"

"He owns Waves."

Katie held her cheeks. "Of course! While I was getting my hair done at Silvo's last week, I skimmed an article about that site's meteoric rise. Interesting stuff. The color shots of the CEO were even better. The article ended by saying he might pose nude for a calendar to support a charity he's behind."

Arranging a choice of table gifts for her soon-to-arrive client, Scarlet refused to acknowledge the heat flaring in her chest…at the tips of her breasts. But she couldn't shake the image of Daniel McNeal sans clothes. Below his folded cuffs, his forearms were strong and brushed with a healthy tan. The exposed vee below the solid column of his neck had revealed a tantalizing hint of the hair and hot flesh that lay beneath. Jeans suited his rebel-with-a-cause air. She wouldn't—*shouldn't*—imagine how delicious he'd look out of them.

"What was he doing here?" Katie was asking.

Dismissing the tug low at her core, Scarlet positioned a floral arrangement on the table. "Wouldn't you assume he was here about a wedding?"

"Sure, but not his."

"Because there's been no public announcement?"

"Because if he was going to take the plunge, make the big merger, he wouldn't have looked at you the way he did."

Darting a glance toward the door, Scarlet lowered her voice. "Do you want someone to hear?"

When Katie reached for a jelly bean from her glass bowl stash at the table's end, Scarlet reminded her, "Not the pink ones."

Popping a white and a green, Katie mumbled and chewed. "Know what you need?"

Scarlet took the pink bean lying on top. "I have a feeling you're about to tell me."

"You need to forget yourself and all the obligations—real and imagined—hanging around your neck, even for a week. It'd only take that long."

"That long to do what?"

"To realize that there's more to life than what's expected. Or that what you've been raised to believe won't necessarily make you happy. And that's all I'll say on the matter." Katie crossed her heart to seal the deal before she asked, "Ariella's not around?"

"She's working from home today."

"First that huge 'the president's your dad' announcement, then weeks of the media sticking their big fat noses in her business... Far as I'm concerned, Ariella's a rock. I'd be an agoraphobic mess by now."

"It must be tough." Slipping the jelly bean between her lips, Scarlet chewed thoughtfully. "Way worse than tough."

"Wonder when the DNA tests will be back."

"Soon now, I imagine."

On the samples table, Scarlet's smartphone buzzed. She opened the text. Her friend's ears must have been burning.

Need 2 see u, Ariella's message read. Test results just in.

Two

Morgan Tibbs swung her attention from the pages of *Time* to her boss when he strode into the penthouse suite. As Daniel continued on to the room that served as his office whenever they were here in D.C., which was often enough to warrant a long-term lease on this and another suite as well as an on-site vehicle, his executive personal assistant tracked his progress.

"You said you'd be out the rest of the day," Morgan said.

"Come in here for a moment, will you?"

He was standing by the wall-to-wall windows, which overlooked Connecticut Avenue and, in the distance, the Washington Monument obelisk when Morgan entered the room. She pretended to shudder.

"Wow. Am I seeing right? You look stressed?"

"I met a woman today."

Morgan waited.

"And?"

"There's something different about her."

His assistant with the attitude clutched at her heart. "I didn't think it would ever happen. I told you we weren't interchangeable."

"I've never said that. Particularly not about you."

"Me aside, let's face it. You might be Einstein where IT is concerned but you're a freshman as far as intimate relationships go. Four weeks seems about your limit."

"If something's not working, why drag it out?"

"He says, leaving behind a string of women with bittersweet stars in their eyes."

Daniel faced her. "But you've never had stars in your eyes where I'm concerned, have you, Morgan?" He headed for his desk. "At the risk of sounding full of myself, why not?"

Daniel guessed Morgan's ancestry lay in the East. Her hair was gleaming and straight, like a sheet of darkest silk. She was petite with dainty hands, a round face and an impressive IQ that gave his own impressive score a run for its money. She also possessed a telepathic ability to predict his needs precisely, which was the reason she accompanied him everywhere. Rarely was she taken aback. Now, however, genuine shock widened her almond-shaped eyes.

"You're my boss," she said. "Being attracted to you would never enter my head."

"Same here."

"Because of that extra ear in the middle of my forehead, right?"

"All I'm saying is a man knows when there's a mutual connection. He feels that spark. The simmer of primal heat."

She knitted her fine, dark eyebrows together. "Maybe you should talk to a boy buddy about this."

"No. I need a female's take."

Pushing out a breath, she crossed over to him, her designer combat trousers rustling as she took a seat. "So, you met a woman."

"I asked her out to dinner. She declined."

Morgan grinned. "I'll put out a press release."

"She wanted to say yes, but something held her back. She was trying her best to be cool about it. Dismissive. But I'm not mistaken. Those sparks were firing."

He recalled the way Scarlet Anders had looked at him, almost fearful but hungry, too. What was the problem? She didn't like his cologne?

"My best guess," Morgan said, "is that she's either seeing a guy or getting over one."

"Attached or burned...I see." He absorbed the opinion, then went on. "I have her number. Business number at least." He drummed his fingers on the desk, made a decision, then reached for the phone. "I'll call her."

Morgan cringed. "If she said no, that move could feel a little stalkerish."

"I don't stalk. It'd be a follow-up."

"Uh-huh." She stretched out her legs and her Doc Marten heels dug into beige plush pile. "Who is she?"

Daniel filled Morgan in. She already knew about Max and Caroline Cranshaw tying the knot; part of his reason for being in D.C. was to personally congratulate the couple and offer his support before the big day. Morgan hadn't known about his planned visit to DC Affairs, however. When he'd finished telling her about his meeting with Scarlet, his assistant blinked twice.

"Let me get this straight. You want to help a professional wedding planner plan a wedding?"

"You're on my side, remember?"

"Fine." She shrugged as if this most difficult problem had an easy solution. "Next time you meet up with Max Grayson and his fiancée, ask a few questions about your Scarlet. If she and Caroline Crawshaw are good friends, as you say they are, she'll gush with information."

The cogs began to whir, and his smile grew and grew.

"Very crafty, Ms. Tibbs."

"I learned from the best."

"Now you're accusing me of being shrewd?" Tipping back, he thatched his fingers behind his head and put his loafers up on the desk, crossing one ankle over the other. "Need I remind you that I'm the poster boy for Free and Easy."

"Or that's what you'd like everyone to believe, including yourself."

His grin wavered. Sometimes he wondered if his assistant knew him a little *too* well.

"Now that we have your social life sorted," Morgan went on, "you need to know who called today. It's not public knowledge yet, but apparently a congressional committee has been formed to investigate concerns regarding hacking into private computer systems and phone networks during the presidential campaign."

"Which resulted in the president's paternity question." Daniel straightened and set both feet on the floor. "Why am I not surprised?"

"They want you to return their call as soon as possible."

An army of ants crawled up Daniel's back and he shuddered. "I don't like this cloak and dagger stuff."

"Then you'd better get the hell out of Dodge." When his frown didn't ease, she sighed and pushed to her feet. "You're the current Mr. Big of the IT world. They want to pump you for information on the basics as well as possible dangers of hacking they'd rather not even think about. Most importantly, they're hoping you can tell them who might be behind it all." She headed out. "I'll get that commission representative back on the phone."

"Hang on to that thought." Daniel reached for the office extension. "The White House might be digging for clues, but I have a pressing matter of my own to clear up first."

He'd decided to follow Morgan's sound advice regarding Scarlet Anders. He wouldn't call her. He had a far better idea.

Scarlet greeted Ariella Winthrop at her Georgetown town house with a huge I'm-here-for-you hug, then quickly shut the door.

After receiving Ariella's text message, Scarlet had called her right back. Her friend had wanted a hand to hold when she read the paternity results. Rather than meet at Ariella's house or the office, where the chance of media hounds skulking around was higher, they'd agreed to meet at Scarlet's home as soon as possible.

Now Ariella reached to take her friend's hand at the same time Scarlet spotted the envelope.

"When I lost my adoptive parents in that accident," Ariella said, lifting that envelope to her chest, "I missed them so much I prayed that a miracle would bring them back. Now I'm finally facing the prospect of knowing my biological father. Hopefully having a relationship. I can't get my head around the fact that man might be the president of the United States."

"You still haven't spoken with Ted Morrow?"

"Only his office. It's all very clinical. Respectful but with an undercurrent of 'tread carefully.' As if I'm anyone to be afraid of."

Except where the president's popularity polls were concerned, Scarlet thought. This situation should have had nothing to do with politics but some were of the opinion private skeletons in the closet made for the juiciest scandals. In this day and age of sharing everything with everyone on sites like Waves, it seemed that nothing remained sacred, including an individual's feelings.

Scarlet asked, "How are you holding up?"

"I have so many nerves bouncing around in my stomach, I feel sick."

"Come in. Sit down. We'll open it together."

Arms around each other's waists, Scarlet guided her friend through to the living room. They'd spent months here together in this very room, going over plans for their business, discussing individual strengths, hopes, fears. Both women had been so anxious—and thrilled—when the doors to DC Affairs had finally opened.

Since then, they'd learned together and, like anyone, had made their share of mistakes. But they hadn't quarreled once and, consequently, their friendship had grown even stronger. There were times they laughed and times where one or the other had needed support.

Times like this.

The women took a seat close together on a sofa positioned adjacent to the piano and directly opposite the fireplace. On the mantel, Scarlet's parents smiled out from the heart of a white-gold frame. The three Anderses were cut from the same cloth—proud, strong and loving.… Although her mother could be a little, well, overzealous sometimes. She was pleased her daughter was dating a Matheson, and didn't lose an opportunity to remind Scarlet of such.

Still, if there was one thing Scarlet could be certain of, it was her roots. Today, Ariella's journey of fitting together missing pieces of her own past might truly have begun.

Staring down at the envelope, Ariella siphoned back a big lungful of air, then blew it shakily out.

"I haven't stopped looking in the mirror, at photos," she said, "wondering if there's a resemblance. I find myself smiling, hoping that it's him. Then I wince thinking how he might react if it's true. And most of all…" She pushed out a sigh. "Most of all I wonder about my mother. I'm actually grateful the press dug around the president's earlier life and found out who his high school sweetheart was. We know she left for Ireland years ago, but why can't Eleanor Albert be found now? Why did she give me up for adoption? I need to know why she and Ted Morrow broke up. Was it because of the baby? Because of me?"

"At least you have a name now," Scarlet said gently.

Ariella nodded, pushed out another shuddery breath, then shunted the envelope across to her friend.

"Will you do it?" she asked. "I'm shaking so much, I might tear it."

A withering feeling fell through Scarlet's center. The country was on tenterhooks waiting for these results. Now was one of those pivotal moments in history, and she'd be one of the first to know the truth.

Scarlet pried open the flap, slid out the record, ran her eye down the page. Lots of stats, but the information Ariella so desperately sought was outlined at the top.

"It says there's a 99.99999% probability of paternity." Lowering the page, Scarlet met her friend's glassy gaze. "That means Ted Morrow is your father. Ariella, you're the president's daughter."

"There's been a whisper. A congressional committee's been formed to look into this hacking business."

Receiver pressed to an ear, Daniel smirked at Max Grayson's announcement. "I was privileged to have received a personal invitation to the proceedings."

The laptop sat at one side of his desk. Daniel opened the most recent Waves feed, scrolled down, but no word of a committee had gone viral yet…although every man and his dog was discussing ANS's paternity accusation against President Morrow.

"The White House must be revved up on high preparing to hunt down anyone connected with tampering with private phone and computer lines to obtain the information." Max circled back. "Did you just say someone from this committee called you?"

"Affirmative. Can you give me some background? I know that Brit, Colin Middlebury, was lobbying for the U.S. to form a tech treaty with the U.K."

"Middlebury got the treaty through with Senator Tate's support. Word is, Middlebury's family has been stung by hacking jobs in Britain. He's passionate about hauling guilty parties out into the open and bringing them to justice." Max's voice lowered. "If they've asked you to appear, be sure to take your lawyer."

Daniel groaned. "And a joyous time was had by all."

"Don't joke about it. They'll pick your brains till they bleed about the fundamentals and specifics of the nebulous art of hacking. Whether you might have any ideas or leads on any likely suspects."

"I'm not in the business of consorting with people who get their jollies from illegal activity."

"But you are a world leader in IT. So, any ideas?"

"You mean aside from the obvious?"

"ANS." Max hissed down the line. "That network's ethics are questionable, and that's being kind. If there's no political dirt around, they'll rustle up some grist and churn out their own. I can tell you, given Cara's condition, she's pleased to be away from all that."

Daniel remembered their conversation when Max had shared his engagement news. His pregnant fiancée had walked away from her high-pressure position in the White House Press Office to work with her party-planning friends in a PR capacity. This was his in.

"Actually, I met Cara's friend today," he said.

"Ariella?"

"Scarlet Anders. I dropped into DC Affairs."

"You should have called. Cara doesn't go in every day,

but she'd have been happy to show you around. What were you doing there?"

"Being a good best man."

"You mean looking into organizing stuff? Guess we'll have to start thinking about cars and suits and those pre-ceremony drinks."

Sure. Not that *he* drank. Ever.

"She's an interesting woman."

"Scarlet? Cara adores her," Max confirmed. "Although, between you and me, she can be a little snooty. You won't catch Scarlet Anders putting a debutante foot out of place. Her parents are pillars of Washington society and their little girl is a carbon copy of her folks. First Lady material, that one."

Daniel grimaced. A life of unerring duty and plastic smiles? "Maybe she needs someone to show her how to loosen up."

"That someone being you?"

"I asked her out to dinner. She said no."

"We're paying DC Affairs to do a job. Scarlet wouldn't dream of mixing business with pleasure."

"I thought she might be involved with someone."

"Cara and I went out with her and a high-profile suit named Everett Matheson recently. Starchy personality to go with his impeccable pedigree."

"Is it serious?"

"They were both so concerned about making sure they used the right fork and acknowledged the right people, I couldn't tell."

"But no kissing? Holding hands? Rubbing noses?"

"She straightened his tie at one stage."

Daniel grinned. "You won't turn me off. You know how I love a challenge."

"I know how much you like *laid-back* and that, my friend, is something Scarlet Anders is not. Poised, admired, even snobbish, yes. She'd rather stab herself in the heart than pick her teeth in public."

Daniel thought about how he loved to shovel popcorn while watching a game. How he abhorred routine and attending functions because it was expected. He recalled how he got off on revving his motorbike to the max down the Great Ocean Road when the urge struck. Then he imagined Scarlet sitting behind him wearing Catwoman leathers, clinging on, arms lashed around his waist with the wind making flying ribbons of her long red hair. At least he guessed that, when it was free, her hair was long. Past her shoulders. Maybe halfway down her back.

He smiled.

Bet it felt like satin.

Daniel pushed to his feet. "Think I'll ask her out again."

"You're incorrigible."

"I have a good feeling."

Max chuckled. "Don't say I didn't warn you."

Max had to answer another incoming call and the men signed off. Daniel dialed the number for the committee and, putting justice rather than his own aversions first, agreed to come in when requested. Then for the next couple of hours he battled over that other, far more enticing matter.

He'd decided against calling Scarlet. He didn't like the idea of showing up again unannounced. He'd had an idea earlier. Around three, he had it perfected.

He'd heard Max about the Everett Matheson character being a contender. But Scarlet wasn't spoken for, and Daniel's fair and reasonable barometer said, *Go for it*. She might be playing near impossible to get but she was definitely interested.

After some research on the web, he chose a florist located near Scarlet's place of business.

"I need some flowers delivered as soon as possible today,"

he told the woman who answered the phone. "An added charge is no problem."

"I'll deliver them myself," she assured him. "What kind?"

"They're called heaven's trumpets." To complement an angel. When a silence followed, he prodded. "Something wrong?"

"You're aware that plant is highly toxic."

Bending close to his laptop's screen, he scrolled down, read on. *Damn.* "I missed that."

"They are beautiful blooms, distinct perfume—"

"And poisonous." He couldn't see Scarlet Anders chewing on a petal, still…not the message he wanted to send.

The woman went on, "Could I suggest something more traditional. Perhaps roses."

"I don't do traditional."

Unless…

As the idea took shape, Daniel explained what he had in mind and, laughing, the woman on the other end of the line assured him that his instructions would be followed to a T. When details for the bouquet were set, he gave his name and credit card details as well as Scarlet's name and address.

The woman coughed as if she'd lost her breath. His jaw shifted. "You okay?"

With a smile in her vaguely familiar voice, the woman replied, "Mr. McNeal, I'm positively floating."

Three

When Ariella stopped shaking and had gathered herself enough to be on her way—taking with her the paper that confirmed she was, indeed, the president's daughter—Scarlet traveled back to work.

On the road, her mind kept wheeling back over the fact that Ted Morrow would have received the positive results by now, too. Scarlet pitied Ariella the media attention that would multiply tenfold now, particularly from the hyenas at ANS who had first broken the paternity scandal wide open. Hopefully some good would come from all this, though. A father and his daughter being reunited for one. And maybe the story wouldn't end there....

The president was a bachelor. Wouldn't it be wonderful if, after all these years, Ted Morrow and Ariella's mother were not only reintroduced but married? What an amazing ceremony *that* would be. And, after a lifetime of separation, Ariella would have her biological family back again.

For the rest of the afternoon, Scarlet was kept busy with inquiries as well as putting the finishing touches to a client's big day to be held at the Washington National Cathedral. Girls dreamed of one day walking down the aisle of that gothic-inspired masterpiece. The famed Canterbury Cathedral had supplied the stone from which the pulpit was carved. Memorials to persons and events of national significance were on display, including statues of presidents Washington and Lincoln. Seals were embedded in the narthex's marble floor and the nave was lined with state flags.

Heading into her office, Scarlet smiled.

Only in D.C.

But before any bride and groom could consider the National Cathedral as a venue, at least one of three strict requirements must be met, which Everett's family did. The bride or groom could have an alumnus connection with a cathedral school. The bride or groom or immediate family member could be employed by the cathedral. Or the bride, groom or immediate family member might be a prominent donor or significant volunteer. Apparently Everett and his parents donated regularly and extremely well when the plate was passed around.. He'd even mentioned the night before, after the proposal, about submitting a request for him and Scarlet to be married there. At the time Scarlet had thought not of herself but of her parents; how ridiculously proud they would be. Then she'd imagined her mother poring over the arrangements, particularly the highly prized invitations list. Faith Anders would want to include everyone who mattered. Everett's parents would feel the same way.

Given her parents' social standing, Scarlet had always known that her own special day would be big, with every convention not only followed but prominently displayed. She'd organized enough of those weddings to know they could be exhausting for the bride. But then anything worthwhile usually was.

As Scarlet packed up for the day, her thoughts wandered more. What kind of a wedding would Daniel McNeal want? Something casual. Even zany, perhaps. Certainly nothing that would suit her needs or taste. Anyway, Mr. McNeal didn't strike her as the marrying kind.

About to head out, she stopped to catch a private call on her cell.

"Ariella rang," Cara Cranshaw began. "She left a message. I only got ahold of her now. She told me the results."

"I wonder when the paparazzi will get wind of the news. No offense."

"Believe me, Max doesn't like the way this was handled by the press any more than we do."

Max Grayson had been a reporter before switching to an off-camera role.

"How was Ariella when she left you?" Cara asked.

"Resigned to the fact that nothing will ever be the same." Scarlet closed her office door behind her.

"I asked her over. I figured she might need some company but she said she'd rather be alone tonight."

Scarlet had thought about offering her friend company, as well. "I'll text and say we're here if she needs us."

"What are you doing tonight?" Cara asked. "I'm staying at Max's place, but he's working until late. Your man's out of town for a few days, isn't he?"

Moving toward the front reception area, Scarlet's thoughts skidded to a halt. By "your man," Cara had meant Everett, but for some crazy reason Daniel McNeal's face had flashed in her mind. As if he were standing before her now, with that crooked grin and sexy dark blond bed-hair, awareness rippled through her, making every one of her extremities tingle.

Totally inappropriate.

Back straight, she continued on her way, picking up the thread of the conversation.

"One of Everett's New York clients needed some figures evaluated."

"Why don't you come over, then?" Cara said. "We can dabble with details for the reception. I'm still torn about a color scheme."

Scarlet hesitated. Now that Ariella didn't want company tonight, she'd half thought about forgetting the outside world for a while and chilling out with a glass of wine. But she adored Cara's company. And aside from the fun of discussing her friend's wedding, she did have her own bit of news to share.

Or should she wait for the ring to be on her finger? For Everett to return from New York… There really wasn't any rush.

"Sure." Scarlet breezed through the foyer. Although Cara and Max as good as lived together now, Cara had kept her great loft apartment so Scarlet hadn't needed to visit Max's penthouse yet, but she knew the address from the Cranshaw-Grayson Wedding file. "See you in an hour."

Lee, their effervescent receptionist, had already left for the day. But halfway to the door, something on the front counter caught Scarlet's eye and dragged her all the way back. A dozen roses—a mix of yellow, coral and peach—sat perfectly arranged in a round glass bowl. Inhaling, Scarlet sighed at their exquisite perfume. Her fingertips brushed the velvet-soft petals. But the best part—the thing that set this bouquet above any other—was the highly original add-in. Perched atop an artificial stem sat a toy animal. A marsupial to be exact.

A boxing kangaroo dressed in a tuxedo and a big black bow tie.

At home, Scarlet ran a deep bubble bath and put on a favorite classical CD. While she soaked, she reconsidered Ariella's situation, then dwelled again on the thousand and one details relating to the cathedral wedding they were planning. But her thoughts kept swerving back to Daniel McNeal, his kangaroo-topped bouquet and the way he'd caught her in his arms when that fateful misstep had sent her toppling off her ladder.

Sinking lower in the scented suds, she recalled how his blue gaze had burned, leaving her lips feeling scorched and her equilibrium in tatters. She'd been attracted to men before but never in this quivery, syrupy way that left her short of breath and, for the first time in her life, reassessing who she was. Even doubting what she wanted.

Was this sudden irrational attraction a common enough case of cold feet?

As far as Scarlet was concerned, aside from having children, getting married was the most important event of a person's life. Being a little anxious was only natural even though she'd known Everett for over a year. On all fronts they got on well. Most importantly, she loved him. Not dizzy, cry-myself-to-sleep-over-you love but rather an appropriate, stable kind of affection. Which was a far cry from her intense schoolgirl reaction to Daniel.

What was love—a sound marriage—based on, anyway? Respect and support of mutual goals. Not wild, lust-driven emotions for someone who was so obviously her opposite. Daniel exuded a blistering energy that would likely set off fireworks in any woman's central nervous system. He was insanely handsome, charismatic and confident. From what she'd seen of it, his tall, toned physique was exceptional. His personality was cheeky. Intriguing.

Like his see-all blue eyes.

Out of the tub and drying off, Scarlet crossed into her bedroom's walk-in closet. Her fingers skimmed business skirts and after-five dresses. When she paused at a pair of jeans, she remembered the way the denim had hugged Daniel's muscled thighs today and a breath fluttered in her throat. She didn't often wear jeans. Cruisy Daniel McNeal might suggest she didn't wear them often enough. But she wasn't dressing for him tonight. Or any other night, for that matter.

Before pulling on a light angora sweater and black tailored pants, she called a cab and pulled a bottle of Chablis from the fridge. Because of her condition, Cara wouldn't drink but Scarlet could go one or two herself tonight.

Scarlet soon arrived at Max Grayson's address. Her friend answered the door to the penthouse with a welcoming smile.

"Come on in," Cara said, stepping aside. "I was about to call you."

"I'm a little late. I indulged in a lovely long bath...."

Stepping over the threshold, Scarlet's words trailed off. A voice was filtering out from the living room into the foyer. A man's voice. Deep. Rumbling. She frowned.

Cara had said Max would be working late.

Then another male voice replied to the first and Scarlet's heart leaped to her instantly clogged throat. That accent was unmistakable. What was *he* doing here? This was supposed to be a quiet girls' night in, not a foursome, and certainly not with Daniel McNeal.

What would she say if he mentioned those flowers? Worse, how would she react if he smiled at her that certain unsettling way? She'd bet her town house he'd find an excuse to prowl into her off-limits personal space.

Scarlet took a shaky step back.

She had to go.

"You said Max was working late."

"He surprised me."

"I don't want to interrupt."

Laughing softly, Cara urged her friend forward. "You're not interrupting, silly. In fact, there's someone here we'd like you to meet."

Scarlet's thoughts and stomach lurched. She needed an

excuse. Needed to get out of here fast. But Cara had a hold of her arm now and, with each doubtful step, those voices grew louder, clearer. A series of internal brushfires ignited, pumping forbidden heat through her veins, leaving her feeling flushed and all the more flustered. Then she and Cara stood beneath an arch that led into the living room and two pair of eyes glanced their way.

She was vaguely aware of Max's smile, his standing to greet her and saying hello. She was a thousand times more attuned to the presence of that other man. As Daniel's lidded gaze embraced hers, she was consumed by sensations that were so powerful and bright she felt as if she'd been struck by a bolt of lightning.

Cara introduced her. "Daniel McNeal, I'd like you to meet a dear friend, Scarlet Anders."

With a knowing grin, Daniel languidly pushed to his feet. "We've met."

"You have?" Blinking, Cara's gaze shifted back and forth between the two of them. "Where? When? You've only been in town a day."

In her daze, Scarlet recognized that Daniel had swapped jeans for custom-made dark trousers and a crisp white shirt. As he strolled over, his polished lace-ups gleamed in the track lighting and a gold cuff link flashed as he extended a big bronzed hand. Without thinking, she accepted the gesture and that lightning bolt struck again, zapping and sizzling up her arm until, with a starburst, it hit her chest as well as a little south of her navel. It didn't help when his fingers wrapped around hers and squeezed just a little like they had earlier that day.

"We met this morning," he said, then proceeded to fill his audience in on how he'd shown up at DC Affairs and saved her from that stepladder fall.

"Thank God you were there," Cara said while Scarlet pried

her gaze away from Daniel's to concentrate on the fact that he still held her hand. Bringing herself back to the conversation, she gently pulled her hand away.

"I've already thanked Mr. McNeal for his help."

"Mr. McNeal?" Cara pulled a wry face. "You're not at the office now. Let me take that bottle of wine. Max, can you pour Scarlet a drink? Something with bubbles to celebrate friends coming together."

Scarlet's attention skirted around Daniel's frame. Max was headed for the bar, but he looked quizzically over his shoulder at his two guests, as if he knew something he shouldn't. Had Daniel already confided in his friend the fact that they'd met? That he'd asked her out to dinner? If that were the case, surely Max would have mentioned she was dating someone....

Although Max had only once seen her with Everett, and her date had spent half the time away from their table on his cell. Understandable. Even forgivable. Everett's services were in high demand.

Daniel was escorting her to the two sofas in the living room. Cara had lowered onto the three-seater. Max, having handed over a chilled glass of champagne to their latest guest, was joining her. Left with no choice, Scarlet sank onto the two-seater, and Daniel sat beside her. Finding his glass—containing what looked like a soda—he proposed a toast.

"To rescuing a damsel in distress."

Raising her own lime soda, Cara beamed. "Hear, hear. Although I've never known Scarlet to need saving before."

Daniel's brows arched and a sexy bracket formed at one side of his mouth as he smiled. "Is that so?"

"Of all my friends, Scarlet is the one least likely to crumple under pressure."

"Oh, I don't know about that." Scarlet was thinking of Ariella and how well she'd handled the recent media attention. She doubted, put in the same situation, she'd handle that kind of news with anything less than a lock-me-away-for-a-month meltdown.

"Scarlet, honestly." Cara set her glass on the coffee table. "In your world, nothing's ever out of place. You invented the word *poise*."

"Begs the question, doesn't it? What do you do to unwind?" Daniel asked casually while Scarlet, her mind gone blank, clasped her hands in her lap.

To *unwind?* "Well...I, er, like to ski."

"Me, too." Daniel laughed. "On the water, though, not in Aspen."

Scarlet didn't allow herself to imagine him in bathing shorts. Those shoulders, that chest... Lord, she might hyperventilate.

"I like to read and go to the theater," she added.

Daniel considered that, then asked, "How about bikes?"

"I own a bike," she replied, "but I don't get out near enough. Peddling around is good exercise, though."

"I mean motorbikes."

"As long as I've known him," Max said, "Daniel has loved belting down a highway on two wheels."

Scarlet forced a polite smile. "I'm afraid I've never been on that kind of a bike."

"You should try it." Daniel tipped a fraction closer and his intoxicating masculine scent drifted into her system. "I could take you out. Bet you'd like it."

She pinned him with a warning look. "Bet I wouldn't."

"Maybe we should call that cab now," Max pitched in.

Scarlet glanced across. "What cab?"

"When Max showed up with Daniel," Cara said, "and I told them I was expecting you, he suggested we all go out to grab a bite."

Daniel looked at her innocently. "Would you like to come out to dinner?"

She narrowed her eyes at him. "Thank you, no."

"Scarlet, are you feeling all right?"

At the concerned note in Cara's voice, Scarlet preened back her ruffled feathers and remembered where she was, who she was with. She made it a point never to be rude. That only revealed weakness. A lack of self-control.

"I'm fine," she said evenly. "I'm just…not dressed to go out."

Cara waved the excuse away. "You look fabulous, as always."

Cornered, Scarlet took a good long sip of champagne. Cara might not have picked up on the thrust and parry game she and Daniel were playing but, from the gleam in his eye, Daniel McNeal wanted Scarlet to know he was intent on pursuing her. She ought to tell him here and now she was unavailable. In fact, what was stopping her? She didn't need to be gauche and slap him around the head with it. Perhaps if she happened to mention that she was missing Everett.

Even if that wasn't strictly true. Everett hadn't been gone twenty-four hours, and she'd had a pile of other stuff filling her head.

"Scarlet was very helpful today," Daniel was saying.

Her chin tucked in. "I was?"

"When you agreed to work with me on some ideas I'd like to contribute to the wedding," he reminded her.

"I said I'd *look over* your ideas."

"What kind of ideas?" Cara asked.

"A couple of small things," he said, "that won't clash with etiquette or good taste."

Daniel sent Scarlet a mischievous "proud of me?" grin while Cara's eyes shone with affection.

"I'm not the least surprised she made herself available," Cara said. "Scarlet's not only a great friend, she's the best wedding planner around."

Scarlet burned to speak up. Yes, she was Cara's friend and would do anything in her power to make certain her big day was everything it should be, and more. But that didn't equate to spending time with Daniel. He made her feel uncomfortable. Restless. Or was that reckless?

Not herself at all.

Cara pushed to her feet. "I'll just go get my bag."

"Wait for me. I'll grab my wallet and cell phone." Following Cara, Max apologized to his guests, "We won't be long."

Daniel reassured him. "Take your time."

When they were alone, he sat back and simply waited. Eventually, over the lump of irritation building in her throat, Scarlet managed to speak.

"I received your flowers," she told him. "I admit the kangaroo was a novel touch."

"The florist thought so, too."

"By the card, the florist is the woman you met today. Katie. She owns the shop a couple of doors down from DC Affairs."

"Right. Now it makes sense. On the phone she seemed particularly pleased with the order."

Scarlet bristled. *Enough.*

"You need to know." She set her flute down. "I'm seeing someone."

His forehead creased. "Does your florist friend know?"

"She does now."

"I don't see any ring on your finger." When she inhaled a shocked breath, the ruthless slant of his mouth faded and his shoulders rolled back. "So, go ahead and tell me. Are you serious about this guy? And before you answer, I want you to know that I think you're a beautiful, intriguing, slightly priggish woman, who I am thankful has finally agreed to come out this evening."

"I did not agree to go out with you." She blinked. "Did you say priggish?"

"Don't take it as an insult. Prim is highly attractive on you. Although I can't help but want to see more of your less guarded side."

"I'm not guarded." Crossing her legs, she refolded her hands on her lap. "I'm careful."

His voice lowered. "I think you should come for a ride with me. I sense there's a whole lot more to Scarlet Anders and I want the chance to get to know every bit of her."

As his gaze roamed her face and her throat, a dangerous fizzy feeling sailed through her body, calling her, drawing her, and as if tugged by an invisible string she tipped a fraction closer, too. Then one corner of his mouth curved up and, appalled by her behavior—at her craving—she jerked back again.

"Don't look at me like that. You're too…" She emptied her lungs, took another shallow breath. "You're too close."

"It's going to be difficult," he said. "Sitting beside you all night. Telling myself that I shouldn't."

"Shouldn't what?"

In that deep drugging voice, he murmured, "Kiss you, of course."

Watching the color and emotion in Scarlet's eyes deepen and grow, Daniel followed the instinct that told him to lean in. He'd thought about her surrender—about this moment— all day long. Now he was a heartbeat away from claiming that much anticipated kiss.

Then a familiar voice rang out.

"Did we interrupt something?"

Driving down an audible breath, Scarlet sat ramrod straight as they both glanced up to where Cara stood in the adjoining doorway, her expression tinged with curiosity. A second later, she released an understanding grin.

"Are you two going over those ideas of Daniel's?" Cara moved forward. "I cannot wait to hear what they are."

Looking a little unsteady, Scarlet got to her feet. When her leg bumped the table, Daniel caught the slender stem of her glass while she fumbled for words and her usual aplomb.

"Actually, I'm sorry, but I need to go," Scarlet said. "Everett sent a text message. He wants me to call straightaway."

Daniel's jaw tightened. So, when the pressure was on, his angel wasn't adverse to a little white lie.

"Everett?" he asked, knowing full well who he was.

"That's right." Looking down at him, Scarlet added, "Matheson III."

"Impressive name," Daniel drawled.

"He's an impressive man."

Obviously not *too* impressive. He might have taken Scarlet out a couple of times but he hadn't held her attention. And she was the kind of woman who deserved a man's *full* attention, whenever and wherever she pleased. But she obviously felt strongly about dear Everett. He'd be a clod not to acknowledge that now.

Stopping behind the sofa, Cara spoke to her friend. "If you need privacy to call, use the study or my bedroom."

"I could be a while." Scarlet collected her designer tote off the sofa's end and wound the strap securely over her shoulder. "I don't want to hold you all up."

Cara's brow creased in concern. "Must be important."

Scarlet nodded. "It really is."

At the door, she apologized again and she and Cara hugged, after which Max dropped a parting kiss on her cheek and Daniel offered to see her down.

"No need," Scarlet replied firmly. "I'm fine."

"What I mean is, I'm going, too," Daniel explained to Max and Cara. "You guys don't need a third wheel."

"You and Max don't see each other often enough," Cara pointed out. "Of course you're not in the way."

But Max gave his fiancée's shoulder a light squeeze. "Plenty of time," he said. "We'll catch up another time."

During their grindingly slow descent, Scarlet stood on her side of the elevator, Daniel stood on his. The Cold War had nothing on this. Any moment the bomb would hit and all hell would break loose.

"For our friends' sake," she finally said, glaring at the metallic doors, "you and I need to get along. I want to make clear, once and for all, that can't happen if you're constantly hitting on me."

"I know."

She blinked across at him. "You do?"

"As much as I want to pursue this—" and enjoy more of Scarlet's company on more personal terms "—I won't."

Arching a brow, she crossed her arms and looked ahead again. "That's way too easy."

"It's the truth."

Maybe sometime in the future, she'd let down her wall and they'd get together. But right now she was dead-on about their friends coming first and him needing to respect boundaries. By nature he was strong-minded and competitive but never antisocial.

"Think we can start again?" he asked.

"On a just-friends basis?" She rearranged her arms, then wound them tight again. "Frankly, I'm not sure I trust you."

"I'll put together some references."

"Yeah, well, maybe you should."

But when they got off the elevator and journeyed across the building's lobby, her stride became less ardent, her expression less pained.

"If Cara trusts Max and Max trusts you," she said as he

opened the foyer's glass door for her, "I guess I can cut you some slack and move on."

Pleased, he moved with her out into the evening air, which smelled of a change on the way. As a young couple walking their black schnauzer strolled by and a rain cloud swept over the full moon, Daniel tipped an imaginary cap.

"I'll be seeing you, then."

Scarlet surrendered a small but genuine smile. "No doubt."

He headed for the parking lot next door. Rounding the corner, he flicked a glance back. He'd expected to see her heading off to find her own car. Instead, she was standing on the curb, flagging down a cab. Pulling up, he set his hands low on his hips as the odd spot of rain hit his head. The cab sailed past. A moment later, so did another. When the raindrops grew heavier, Daniel walked back.

She was fishing around in her tote as he joined her. Startled, her focus kicked up.

"Daniel. I thought you'd gone."

He hooked a thumb toward the parking lot. "My car's that way."

"I'm more than capable of taking care of myself."

"This one's nonnegotiable. Our friends would never forgive me if they knew I left you standing here alone, waiting—" he fanned out his palms, studied the sky "—with the clouds about to let loose into the bargain."

"If Cara knew the circumstances—"

"She'd tell you to set pride aside and take the lift." With a flourishing wave, he indicated the way to his car. "Your gilded carriage awaits."

She looked set to argue but then a sudden wind picked up and she saw reason. Sliding the strap of her tote back up on her shoulder, she headed off. Daniel fell in step beside her.

Soon they were nestled in his vehicle's bucket seats and Daniel ignited the engine. He set the wipers on low and, after she supplied an address, he pulled out. During the next few minutes, her frostiness thawed more. She even started a conversation, but Daniel assumed it was to be polite more than anything.

"Do your family live in Australia?" she asked.

"Dad's in Sydney. Foster dad, actually," he corrected himself, then added, "My mother died some time ago."

"Oh, Daniel, I'm sorry. She would've been proud of your success. Were you very young?"

"Old enough to remember," he said, swallowing the pit that swelled whenever he thought of those early years, of what had happened and the price they'd all paid. Not a subject he ever elaborated on. Not with his closest friend. Not with anyone. Scarlet, of course, wasn't to know that.

"What about your father?" she asked. "Your biological dad. Hope I'm not prying."

He increased the wiper speed. "It's a topical question, given Ariella Winthrop's situation. Guess the verdict will be out soon there."

"Guess so."

Daniel slid a look across at her. Eyes on the road, Scarlet had her lips pressed together. Did she know something most of the world didn't? Ariella would want to share the results of that paternity test with her closest friends, but Scarlet obviously wasn't the type to break a confidence. Full credit to her.

"Either way, that story will give the media grist for a good while to come," he said.

"You're in the information-sharing business, too," she pointed out.

"But Waves truly is about freedom of speech. Everyday people like you and I get to decide what needs to be discussed."

"You class yourself as *ordinary?*"

"Just a regular bloke."

"Great to know obscene wealth hasn't affected you. We'll ignore the fact you're driving a Lamborghini."

With no traffic in the near vicinity, he changed gears and showed his passenger—for a few gravity-challenged seconds—why he was in love with this baby. When he dropped speed again and Scarlet's hands released their death grip on her thighs, he asked, "What about your family?"

"I'll tell you if you promise not to do that again."

He changed down another gear.

"They live in Georgetown, too," she said.

"Not too close for you?"

"We're a close family. In a healthy way. I make my own decisions. You know. Run my own life."

He chuckled. "Don't try so hard to convince me."

She fell quiet before adding, "Truth is…sometimes they do jump in with an opinion. But I guess most mothers are like that. Overly protective."

He inhaled deeply, then swallowed that damn ache again.

The GPS gave a few more instructions before he pulled up outside a block of upmarket town houses. The rain had stopped so he shut down the wipers. When he left the engine running, however, she seemed surprised.

"You're not seeing me to the door?"

"You don't want me to."

"Wow. You really are trying." Then she cocked her head. "Unless this is a reverse psychology thing where pulling back is supposed to draw me deeper into your web."

He held up his hands. "No webs. I didn't even see the latest *Spider-Man* flick. Yet."

"I've seen it twice. Right through to the very last credit."

"Well, a movie's not over until you've scanned the hundred names under visual effects."

"Now you're mocking me."

"Never."

She tried to hide a grin. "And here I was thinking you were the type who enjoyed getting a rise out of poor unsuspecting folk like me."

"Only if I'm sure they won't belt me."

"Then I should warn you I have a power right hook."

"Which is why I have only the utmost respect for you."

That twinge of a grin grew. "You do, huh?"

"Yeah." He paused. "I really do."

Her eyes were so bright. In the light filtering through her window, her face appeared almost luminous. Free of pretense. Even vulnerable.

Then, as if realizing that vulnerability, Scarlet's smile faded. At the same time, the space separating them seemed to shrink. That sense of sharing—of connecting—changed… spiraled wider, tunneled deeper. And then he was looking at her in a way he'd vowed that he wouldn't.

The tips of his fingers curled around the leather of the steering wheel. He wouldn't act on the need. Even when that superior force building inside of him was so strong…like a big wave curling over his head, pushing him forward, giving him no choice but to leave his sense of reason behind in the wash.

But in his heart of hearts, Daniel knew. Logic had never been the issue here. Not for either of them.

He edged closer.

When his mouth slanted over hers, her eyes drifted shut and those sweet lips parted on a sigh. Any second, he expected her to pull back. Slap his face. But as one heartbeat bled into the next, she only dissolved against him more as if she wanted him to know that she agreed. Despite her objections, this coming together was always going to happen.

His hand found the curve of her neck, the fast but steady beat of a pulse. As his tongue twined with hers, his fingers combed up to cradle the back of her head. They pressed closer, the kiss deepened and his desire to know more—take more—began to burn in his mind like a torch.

When their lips gradually parted, Daniel didn't sense anger. Certainly not disgust. As his gaze searched her face in the shadows, his hand slid around to cup her hot cheek. The pad of his thumb grazed the moist rim of her lower lip. Slowly her heavy-lidded eyes met his.

"You can't ever do that again," she said.

"That would entail never seeing you again."

"If that's what it takes."

He wanted to laugh. Man, was she stubborn.

"I respect that you don't want to blur the lines between personal and your business commitment to Caroline's wedding," he assured her. "And I heard that you've dated some guy with a digit at the end of his name—"

"I'm engaged," she cut in, and that still-wet bottom lip quivered. "To be married."

His gut kicked. That didn't compute. She was kidding. Had to be.

"I don't believe you," he said.

"We haven't made the announcement. Everett only asked me last night. The ring is being resized. It's an heirloom."

Daniel fell away, gripped the wheel. *What the...?*

He growled, "Spare me the details."

But there was one thing he did want to know. Why was she marrying a guy she didn't love? Because, while he'd never experienced that emotion himself, Daniel was bloody sure if he'd wanted someone enough to pop the question, he wouldn't be kissing someone else, not for any reason.

Still, that hardly made him a white knight in this situation. If he hadn't kept on. Hadn't insisted on this lift but had left her to stand there alone in the rain...

Shutting his eyes, he pinched the bridge of his nose.

"I apologize," he said. "I'm not a good loser."

"I'm a far worse fiancée." Her head went back against the rest and, as if she were sick to her stomach, she groaned. "Bad doesn't come close to describing how I feel."

"I take responsibility—"

"No. It's my fault." She looked across at him with a gaze that was turned more inward than out. "You see, when I said I didn't trust you, what I should have said…what I should have understood was that I didn't trust myself."

Scarlet left Daniel with a perplexed look on his face but her own mind strangely clear.

As she closed the car door and walked to her building's entrance, she half wondered if he'd follow. When he didn't, she was grateful for two reasons. Firstly she didn't want that smoldering episode they'd just experienced to have even half a chance of resuming. Ever.

Second—

Now she truly did need to speak with Everett straightaway.

She opened her town house door and, feeling numb, moved to the living room extension. After dialing Everett's cell, she waited calmly to connect. When her call went to voice mail, she wandered across the room and put on a CD. But for once Bach didn't soothe her. If anything the music irritated and unsettled her. She pressed Pause and tried Everett's number again. This time he answered.

"I was on my way out to dinner," Everett said. "My head's buzzing with figures, all of them good." He laughed, a gravelly, breathy kind of sound she realized now she'd never liked. "Goodman asked if I could stay on a few more days. He wants to introduce me to a circle of friends who need some numbers crunched."

"That's all great," she said. "But, Everett, I need to speak with you—"

"I know, I know. I said it'd only be a couple of days but this opportunity is too good to pass up. You know I miss you."

She rubbed her temple. The mother of all headaches had just kicked in.

"It's not that."

"Then you're calling about the ring. Girls and their baubles," he teased. "Don't worry. I left it in my mother's capable hands. She was antsy about having it resized but I told her, it's *me* getting married. Not her."

Scarlet thought of Mrs. Matheson, how her mouth would pinch whenever the older woman greeted her in their lavish home even when Scarlet was unfailingly polite. Perhaps her attitude had something to do with another female stealing her only son.

But maybe Mrs. Matheson was able to sense a problem Scarlet hadn't been aware of—at least, not until today. She not only didn't love Everett, she didn't particularly like him—the way he parted his hair, or spoke to waiters, or always put his work first. When Scarlet thought of it now, she wondered how she managed to mask those feelings. How she'd so blithely dismissed Katie's concern earlier that day.

If Daniel hadn't kissed her tonight, she'd have gone on believing that she'd made a good and wise choice in marrying Everett. To be fair, she'd never paid attention to any other kind of man. Everett was upstanding, predictable. Pious. Like her parents. She had never entertained the notion of embracing something different. She'd never accepted that intensely raw emotions—such euphoric, sizzling sensations—could truly exist.

Everett was still speaking about tax laws and offshore possibilities when she interrupted.

"Everett, I can't marry you."

Stunned silence stretched down the line. Then he cleared his throat. She imagined his elongated nostrils flaring.

"Can you repeat that?"

"I'm sorry. So sorry. I thought I was sure."

"What's changed?"

She thought of her regular diet of classical music, then remembered a kangaroo in a big bow tie. An image of a cathedral wedding appeared in her mind's eye alongside a throbbing motorcycle. Then she imagined a run of business dinners and lonely nights versus the drugging magic of a single kiss.

Shutting her eyes, Scarlet pressed her palm against her pounding temple. "It's not right. *We're* not right."

He exhaled almost patiently.

"You want me to come home?"

"Oh, Everett, that won't change anything."

His voice dropped an octave. "You couldn't wait to tell me to my face?"

"I'd like to think we could still be friends," she said.

But Everett Matheson III had already hung up in her ear.

Four

Amid clusters of tuxedos and glamorous evening gowns, Daniel's senses homed in on her presence with the precision of a heat-seeking missile. The conversation he'd been part of blended in with the background music and tinkle of glassware while his senses sharpened and garnered an inventory of his find.

Her snug bodice topped a fall of gossamer light gold-colored fabric that, slit down the center, pooled in a modest train at her heels. The snow-white layer closest to her skin ended in a cloud at her toes. But that halo of golden-red hair was the showstopper—long, luscious and hypnotic, just as Daniel had imagined it would be.

Conversing with an attentive doyenne of D.C. society, Scarlet Anders must have said something amusing. When her companion threw back her steel-gray chignon and laughed with delight, Daniel felt his own smile spread. A pro at mingling, Scarlet left on a high and bowed off. Daniel also excused himself from his own conversational circle. Sipping from a crystal flute, she cast an inquisitive glance around. When she spotted him strolling toward her, closing the gap, her slender shoulders went up and that beautiful face came alive in a way that made his pulse pound and deepen all the more.

Since that night a week ago, after that unforgettable kiss, he'd kept his distance. Scarlet Anders was betrothed to another man. No matter what his feelings were—the knot in his stomach and warmth in his chest whenever he thought of her—that was the end of it. But here, in public, he wouldn't be so rude as to ignore her. Etiquette decreed he be civil, say hello, exchange pleasantries. Even while his arms already ached to draw her near.

"This is a surprise," he said, stopping before her as the genteel throng hummed around them.

"Daniel." She let out a breath. "I didn't think you'd be into this kind of evening."

"Normally, I'm not a good candidate for these gala events. But tonight is the second reason for my visit to D.C. I'm a long-standing benefactor of this charity."

Her brow furrowed in confusion before she answered her own question. "Right. Youth Rules's head office is here in Washington, but it's an international charity." She seemed to look at him through a slightly different lens. "So, helping youngsters find their way is a cause close to your heart?"

"That—and I'm a sucker for a good auction." He drank in her vibrant smile. "How about you?"

"DC Affairs was hired to look after the hors d'oeuvres, drinks and some frills. A personal invitation showed up in my in-box a month ago, but I'm here more to keep an eye on how everything's running. My parents are around somewhere, too."

Following her lead, Daniel's gaze searched the massive

ballroom. Gold-ridged Corinthian columns delineated the borders of the space. The elevated corniced ceiling had been transformed into a canvas of glittering stars. The waitstaff were dressed in hotel uniforms but not all were delivering nibblies and drinks via the usual means. Some were gliding and sliding around on some kind of roller skates. He tipped his chin at a waitress skillfully rolling past.

"Sneaker skates?" he asked.

"I combined a fluid representation of today's youth," she explained, "with the idea of reaching for the stars as well as the industry and foresight of ancient Greece."

As represented by those columns. "Brave mix." He glanced around again. "But it works."

"Glad you approve."

"So, how's the wedding planning going?" he asked to keep himself from telling her how stunning she looked. As Scarlet might say, *not appropriate*.

"Cara's plans are coming along brilliantly," she said.

"I meant *your* plans."

Her animated expression wilted, then her chin lifted to a proud angle. "As a matter of fact, I broke the engagement off."

Daniel's heart lurched halfway up his throat. Damn. He hadn't seen that coming. Every night this past week, he'd lain awake imagining how Scarlet had ultimately rationalized away the moment they'd shared fogging up his car windows. But it seemed that she'd owned the experience instead.

The society marriage was off. Which meant there was hope for the two of them yet. But no need to gloat or rub it in. As Scarlet had demonstrated a week ago in Max's living room, some situations called for an outright lie.

"I'm sorry to hear it," he said. "Matheson must've been upset."

"I'm sure his ego was dented. I'm just as sure he's getting on with his life."

"Can't keep a good man down?"

Her wry grin said a lot. "How are things in Waves land?" she asked, changing the subject.

"From all accounts, running smoothly. I hope to get back to Sydney next week, then fly back here in time for the wedding."

As best man he'd wanted to add his own special touch to his friend's big day, but knowing how unfavorably Scarlet would view an unorthodox surprise at one of "her" weddings, maybe he should temporarily hang up his nuptial prankster gloves. No teeny cars, their roofs dressed up with giant top hats and tiaras with veils, before swapping the vehicles at the last moment for gleaming Bentleys. No keeping a straight face when presenting a plastic wading pool as a wedding gift at the reception only to have the honeymooning newlyweds' back yard completely renovated to include a magnificent resort style pool, ready for their return.

"Itching to get home to jump on your own set of wheels and belt off down that Great Ocean Road?" Scarlet was asking him.

He narrowed one eye at her, assessing. "You want to do it, don't you. Admit it. You really, really do."

She coughed out a laugh. "I do not."

"First sneaker skates. Soon you'll be stealing peeks at Vespas. Next comes the itch to throw your leg over something more powerful. Something big and hot and smooth."

"Your motorcycle."

"That works, too."

Her eyes rounded. But she quickly gathered herself, brushing an errant wave away from her glowing cheek. "You like to tease, don't you, Daniel."

"Truth is, I like *you,* Scarlet. A lot."

She flicked a half-anxious gaze around the room. "In case you hadn't noticed, we're in public."

"We don't have to be."

Her jaw dropped. But she looked more tempted than outraged. Which fit. She could play coy but she'd ended that relationship because of her feelings for him and, make no mistake, now that she was free, all bets were off.

"We were talking about party planning," she reminded him, diverting the conversation onto higher ground. "This past week, I've cleared my desk to focus solely on Cara and Max's wedding. I've made headway, but there are so many important bits and pieces to see to yet. There's not only all the customs to consider but also family requests." She tilted her head and a diamond drop earring blinked beneath the lights. "You're looking at me strangely."

Intently, hungrily. Yes, he was.

"I think we should forget about work commitments and enjoy the evening," he said.

"I thought we were already doing that."

"I should have said, enjoy it more."

He took her flute and set it on a passing waiter's tray. Then he wound her arm through his and ushered her away, weaving between nattering groups of party guests until they stood among other couples on the dance floor. Beneath the enormous center chandelier, he wove one arm around her slender waist. His other hand twined with hers. Bringing her forearm to rest against his lapel, their bodies warm and close, they began to dance while those stars overhead sparkled in her eyes.

As she moved with him, her gaze never shying from his, he breathed in her heavenly scent. Absorbed the long-anticipated moment. And with each beat of music and strum of his heart, he wanted to confess how very much he needed to up their score from one kiss to two.

"How's your friend Ariella holding up?" he asked instead.

"Remarkably well, considering how the media's been

hounding her. ANS is the worst. The people at the top of that network are shamefully short on scruples. What kind of people enjoy hunting down a fellow human being, goading her, hoping that eventually the pressure will break her down so that they'll get their footage and some reporters will get their five seconds of fame." She shuddered. "Sick."

"Not all reporters are like that." Max—when he had been a reporter—for one.

Her frown faded. "I know. Thank God."

"I take it Ted Morrow and Ariella haven't had a face-to-face yet. When the results of that test are finally released, the White House would want to make sure the president's next move is the right one."

"I can't imagine how it all must be tearing her up inside. Her parents died a few years ago."

"Max mentioned."

"Makes you wonder, doesn't it? How would it feel to have your own father, your own flesh and blood, turn his back on you?"

Daniel's insides kicked and his jaw flexed tight. Outwardly, he raised his brows and replied, "Not good, that's for sure." Keeping his steps in time to the tune, he turned her around. "Have you seen anything you'd like to bid on at the tables?"

She gave an impish grin. "I'm leaning toward that two-week vacation on an exclusive Barrier Reef island courtesy of Anonymous."

"Wonder who that might be."

Her lips twitched. "Hmm. I wonder."

"I'd highly recommend it." And he knew her ideal travel companion. Ah, the fun they could have.

"I've never seen Australia. It seems so far away."

"Don't tell anyone, but it is."

"That big red rock in the center—"

"Uluru."

"Must be an amazing sight."

"Particularly at dawn and dusk. God certainly got His palette right on that one."

Her gaze drifted off to one side as she seemed to imagine experiencing that amazing sight firsthand.

"What's your favorite place back home?" she asked.

"The beaches. The water. I have a yacht moored at Port Hinchinbrook. That's just south of Cairns."

"Barrier Reef territory."

"Ever been snorkeling?"

"My fair skin isn't a fan of UV."

"Imagine hundred-year-old turtles swimming past, close enough to touch. Schools of lightning-fast fish darting before your goggled eyes. Ocean plateaus filled with living, breathing coral. Bright blue and orange and startling green. Something like the color of your eyes." His chin lowered. "And I mean that in a purely nonsexual way."

"Sure you do." Her playful gaze dropped before meeting his again. "But I suppose there's no point avoiding the subject. I can't deny the kiss we shared was rather nice."

"*Nice* isn't the word I'd use."

"Point is," she said, unconsciously squeezing his shoulder, "I am who I am and you are…well, different. We live in different worlds. Might as well be different galaxies."

"Ever heard of the saying 'opposites attract'?"

She plowed on. "You don't like the establishment. As a teen, you rebelled against it. From what I've read these past days, you were on a course destined for crime."

His step almost faltered. Exactly how much research had Scarlet done? How far back had she gone?

"I'm grateful I had someone to help straighten me out."

"Apparently you're a genius and bit of an eccentric," she went on, "who would far rather chill out listening to heavy-metal rock than enjoy a vintage wine before heading off to the opera."

He winced. "You really like opera?"

"All classical music."

"But there aren't any electric guitars."

She sighed at his deadpan as if he'd made her point. "If we did—for whatever reason—get together and…you know…"

The pad of his thumb drew a lazy circle low on her back. "Go on."

"The media would jump on the story. The public consensus would be that Scarlet Anders must have lost her mind partying with a sports-mad, unconventional playboy who, having accrued a massive fortune, only wants to pursue pleasure in any and every way possible."

"That's going too far. I'm not *completely* sports mad."

"When the stardust settles and we return to our separate lives, you'd carry on doing precisely what you do now. But can you imagine the damage to my reputation?"

He thought it over and came to a conclusion of which he was already well aware. "You live your life according to what others think."

"Believe me, around here it matters. DC Affairs's target market is the top-bracket demographic. Why would they entrust their arrangements to a woman who lost her marbles and went on a bender after the breakdown of a steady relationship?"

"Did I mention I have a tattoo? That wouldn't help."

Pushing out a breath, she looked off. "You're not listening."

"I just don't like what I'm hearing."

"Then hear this. No way on this planet would I ever get involved with you. It's not smart."

"And you're a smart girl." Still dancing, he turned her around. "So you don't want to see me again?"

"Other than in relation to Cara and Max, it's best."

"Then I'll bow to your demands."

Her head went back. "You *will?*"

"I may be deemed dangerous and don't know an aria from my—"

"Yep. Got the picture."

"But I am, at heart, a gentleman."

Her eyes twinkled with a knowing smile. "Or that's what you'd have me believe."

"Rarely will I indulge my inner caveman. No matter how much I might want to, I would never go through with the idea of throwing you over one shoulder and dragging my prize out the door and into my animal-fur bed." His fingertips pressed on the small of her back. "Unless you want me to."

And from the increasingly heavy look in her eyes, that was more than a possibility.

In the next breath, however, she shored herself up, reestablishing a suitable space between his hard, muscled chest and her much softer, increasingly more tempting one.

"There's nothing subtle about you, is there?" she said.

"I say what I mean—"

"And I mean what I say."

She broke away and, flustered, walked off. His inner caveman grunted. After running a hand through his hair, Daniel followed.

"You say what you think the establishment wants to hear," he told her as they moved past the other guests. "That's being true to an image, not yourself. That's not being happy."

She stopped to study him. "And I suppose you can make me happy. Destroy my reputation, more like it. I don't think my parents would approve of their only child dating a man who is thinking of posing nude for a high-profile calendar."

"Don't tell me you looked into pre-ordering it."

"I have no desire to see you naked."

He stepped deplorably close and growled, "Liar."

A voice—female, authoritative—joined in from behind.

"Scarlet, would you kindly introduce us to your companion?"

Daniel stepped back. A woman in her fifties, well-maintained, a natural-blonde beauty, was studying him with a mix of curiosity and disapproval. Clearly she'd overheard the end of their conversation. Beside him, Scarlet snapped to attention.

"Daniel McNeal, I'd like you to meet my mother and father, Mr. and Mrs. Anders."

"The founder of Waves. That's quite a donation you've put up for the auction, Mr. McNeal," Mr. Anders said, waving his short glass of Scotch toward the auction tables and too close to Daniel's nose. "I presume you're the anonymous contributor."

"Hope it gets some decent bids," he replied cordially.

"I hear you're a self-made man," Mr. Anders went on.

"With a bit of help at the start."

"Your father?"

Daniel's stomach muscles clenched. That was a good one. His father had helped, all right. Helped ruin a kid's life.

"Actually, it was a physics teacher," Daniel replied evenly. "He spent buckets of time and energy recalibrating my, at times, off-track agenda."

"McNeal…" Mrs. Anders touched her champagne flute to her chin. "Irish, I presume?"

"The joke-telling, river-dancing same, ma'am. An ancestor of mine came out to Australia from there in the nineteenth century."

"Joke-telling and river-dancing." Mrs. Anders's smile was small. "Well, it's certainly good to have pride in one's breeding." Her attention wandered, then her smile took on a genuine light. "Oh, I see the Bancrofts. Scarlet, remember that summer we spent with them and their boy, Thomas, in the Hamptons."

Scarlet puzzled. "You mean when I was nine?"

Mrs. Anders reminisced. "You played Chopin for everyone, remember?"

"I wasn't very good," her daughter admitted.

"You were mature beyond your years," her mother pointed out. "Still are. So clever and responsible." She spoke to Daniel. "Scarlet's father and I are proud of our baby girl."

Scarlet's laugh betrayed a hint of her embarrassment. "Mother, I've been out of pigtails awhile now."

Mrs. Anders tsked. "But we should catch up with the Bancrofts before they head off. Mr. McNeal, please excuse us. Scarlet, join us when you're free. I'm sure Thomas would enjoy seeing you again."

Mr. Anders tipped his head and, when the pair was out of earshot, Daniel voiced a hunch.

"So, your parents know you and Prince Charming III have parted ways."

"Everyone knows."

"Hence the push toward candidate number two." Unsuspecting Thomas Bancroft.

"My parents want to see me happy," she told him. "Settled."

"Or is that shackled?"

Scarlet groaned. "I need some air."

They cut through the crowd to a set of doors. Leaving the natter and music behind, they moved out onto the otherwise vacant balcony. She stopped by the rail and, apparently unaffected by the chill in the air, stared out over the blanket of city lights.

"I don't expect you to understand," she said.

Hell. He didn't want to hurt her, but he couldn't resist saying, "If it's about pedigree and old money, no, I'm afraid I don't."

When she rotated away from the view to face the ballroom

doors, he thought he caught the glimmer of tears in her eyes. It wasn't hard to guess that she felt pulled in a few directions, by her parents and her own stand on what was decent and right. He wasn't helping.

He thought to say something more. Something supportive. Instead, standing behind her, he lightly set a caring hand on her shoulder. After a long moment, the tension bracing her seemed to ease. Exhaling, giving in, she rested back against him. Daniel closed his eyes. Damn, she felt good.

"I don't want to argue with you," she said.

"I don't want to argue with you."

"Let's just agree to disagree."

"Whatever you want."

"Please, don't patronize me."

"You're right. Sorry."

He thought she might have smiled.

"I don't need anyone telling me what's best," she said.

"I take it you're not including your parents in that statement."

"They want me to do well."

"I think you mean marry well."

Growing stiff, she stepped away and faced him. "And what if they do? What's wrong with choosing a life partner who has a higher education, who has family support, who can provide for his spouse and children?"

"Nothing. As long as you're doing it for the right reasons."

She crossed her arms. "Given your reputation for chasing pleasure—and women—I doubt you're anyone to talk about love."

"Doesn't mean I'd sell myself out."

Her face hardened to stone. She took a moment before she spoke. "I believe I've fulfilled my obligations here this evening. Kindly excuse me."

"You don't have to be so polite," he said as she walked away. "Not with me."

"You're wrong. I have to remember myself, *especially* with you."

At DC Affairs, Scarlet was busy in a display room setting up the "paradise island" scene a couple had asked her to develop in anticipation of the real deal when the theme would be recreated at a special venue of their choosing. Palm trees had been strategically placed, blue silk sails hung waiting for a make-believe breeze and glittering starfish lay scattered around a sandstone altar. Once she'd dropped hibiscus blooms beneath the palms and set a veil on the bride mannequin's head, all would be ready for her clients, due in an hour.

Between now and then she'd need to keep herself busy. Keeping her mind and body active helped to ward off those memories that constantly crept in. Since walking away from Daniel at the charity evening night before last, she'd known little peace. Obviously she needed to put his calculated advice—and those self-destructive feelings—behind her. They were from different worlds that could never find a common ground. Not on the most important issues, in any case. She didn't need the angst. That niggling doubt.

Why did he affect her so deeply?

As she shifted the stepladder back, then selected a half dozen flowers off their tray, Scarlet reminded herself that she and Daniel shared a chemistry—an unbelievable, sizzling buzz. That didn't mean she needed to act on that attraction. For one, she didn't do wild weekends filled with what would no doubt prove to be amazing sex with a man she barely knew. She had a reputation and sense of self-worth to maintain.

Second, she was angry with him.

While Daniel might want to persuade her to join him beneath the sheets, his tactics sucked. She had no intention of selling herself out. It was almost enough to make a person side with her mother's lack of tact.

The Anders lineage was reputed to hark back to the *Mayflower*. Sometimes her mother took that as a free ticket to dismiss others less fortunate in that area…someone whose great-great-grandfather might have arrived in his new home chained up in a convict ship's hull, for example. Whatever his roots—and other limitations—Scarlet could admit that Daniel McNeal was an intelligent, articulate, amusing human being. He also happened to have a smile that could light up a small city and, most likely, any woman's heart.

On top of that, Daniel cared enough about his friend Max Grayson to stroll into a place like this. Most guys wouldn't bother themselves with the finer details surrounding anyone's wedding, including their own; on that score, Scarlet spoke from professional experience. Weddings were routinely viewed as women's business. And yet Daniel had put himself out there. He'd wanted to contribute.

As a consequence, they'd met and that introduction had changed her life. If not for Daniel and that extraordinary kiss, she might have gone ahead with her own wedding and made a huge mistake. But that didn't mean she needed to rebound onto Bad Boy personified.

Each display room had a changing facility with a full length, three-sided mirror. Now, as Scarlet lifted the final prop from its box and let the stream of lace drift to the floor, her gaze wandered to her reflection seen beyond the changing room's open door. She wore a white linen dress, purchased recently at a high-end fashion house. Her patent sling-backs were new last week, too. As usual, her hair was coiled up in a professional style that suited the oval shape of her face.

On the day of her own wedding, to whomever the groom may be, would she wear her hair up or let the waves bounce around her shoulders, down her back, as she'd worn it last

Saturday night? She'd always liked the idea of a tiara head-piece to secure her veil. The one she held now had only a simple band of imitation pearls.

Scarlet's gaze went from the veil to her reflection and back again. Her clients weren't due for a while yet and Lee was out on her lunch break, away from the front desk. Anyway, so what if someone caught her in the act. She planned weddings, for Pete's sake. Was around this kind of stuff day in and day out. The question was why she'd never done it before. Girls loved to try on clothes, accessories. Women liked to dress up.

Sometimes they needed to dream.

She unpinned her hair, shook out the waves, then fit the pearl band and its veil atop her own head. After spreading the river of lace out around her feet, she stood tall. As she studied herself in the mirror, a rush of emotion jetted through her system.

In her mind, the wedding dress she wore was long and elaborate, patterned with thousands of beads. Her bouquet was an armful of lilies tied with thick white ribbon that curled down to her shoes. Then, in her mind, the bouquet changed from lilies to a single coral-colored rose, and that bow-tied toy kangaroo appeared, too.

Scarlet frowned at first, but then very slowly smiled.

Mrs. Daniel McNeal.

But bit by bit reality crept back in. Soon only a sensation of feeling strangely out of time and place remained. Life was made up of a chain of choices. One foolish decision could take years to make right; during father-daughter talks, her dad had told her that so many times. Bottom line, she and Daniel were as different as the steamy Congo was from a daisy-covered field. No amount of fantasizing would ever change that.

Slipping off the veil, Scarlet rotated away from the mirror. On her way back to the display, she felt the lace pull and looked back. The last of the train had snagged under one of the ladder's feet.

The wooden floors had been polished the night before. Her new heels lacked tread. As she bent to move the ladder and free the veil, her heel caught the edge of the lace. An instant later, her feet went out from beneath her and, for the second time in a week, she fell.

This time no one was there to catch her.

Five

Daniel entered DC Affairs's reception lounge knowing that coming here for whatever good reason was a mistake. Clearly, Scarlet did not want to see him again. Before he'd left the penthouse, Morgan had said he ought to grow a brain. And yet he felt compelled. His mind was made up.

He needed to speak with Scarlet again.

To say goodbye.

As he crossed to the reception desk, he went through in his mind other loose ends that needed tying up today. Sign off on the Youth Rules auction winners. Confirm his private jet's scheduled time of departure. Say his farewells to Max and Caroline. Of course, he would return to the States to join in their big day, just as he would make himself available when the invitation to testify before that congressional committee landed.

But frankly, this town, its broiling scandals and endless political hoo-ha gave him hives. He'd go nuts dealing with the palaver any longer than necessary. Max—and Scarlet—could have it. Tomorrow he would see the powder-white beaches and smell the eucalypt gum-tree scent of blessed home.

The reception counter was unattended and all seemed deathly quiet. But the open sign was on the door. He'd have expected at least one of the three friends—Ariella, Caroline or Scarlet—to have been on hand. Rubbing the back of his neck, he checked his watch. Maybe he ought to simply leave a note: "Good luck, no hard feelings."

Lots of other feelings, though.

For a bittersweet moment he held on to the image of Scarlet standing in the moonlight. In that goddesslike dress, golden waves mantling her shoulders, he'd had to clench his fists to stop from hauling her back when she'd walked away. But he didn't want to upset her beloved status quo any more than he already had. Hell, he didn't want to hurt her, full stop.

In fact, best he take Morgan's sound advice and get the hell out of here now before he made things worse.

Halfway out the door, an echoing crash filtered down the main corridor and he stopped. Something heavy had smacked the ground. Now an eerie silence followed. He called out, "Everything okay?" When the quiet continued, he followed his gut and set off to investigate.

He strode into the first display room—the one where he and Scarlet had first met. Other than a traditional church steeple and wedding bell display, the room was empty. Then another noise—a metal scraping—reached him from nearby. On a long stride, he entered the next room.

There on the floor she sat propped up on one arm, looking strangely disheveled. That blasted ladder lay on its side near her feet. Her expression was spaced out, heavy-lidded. He raced over and knelt down to support her back.

"Scarlet, are you all right?"

Cringing, she held her crown. "I think…think I hit my head."

He darted a look around. A tapestry-covered chaise waited in one corner of the room. With infinite care, he scooped her up, carried her over and laid her gently down. He crouched beside her.

"What happened?"

She winced and touched her head again. "I don't…don't know."

Over a shoulder, he spotted a river of lace on the floor near the upended ladder. "Did you trip?"

"Maybe. I'm not sure. I'm okay, though." With her eyes closed, she wet her lips and let her head loll to one side. "Just…fuzzy."

He pulled out his cell. "You're getting checked over. You could have a concussion."

"Things are kind of muddled."

"Scarlet. Look at me."

His palm cupping her cheek, he urged her head gently over. Her eyelids fluttered open and evenly dilated pupils focused. Then an entrancing smile spread across her face and, as if the first fingers of dawn had peaked over a new horizon, he grew uncommonly warm inside and smiled right back.

"Hey," she said, "you're really cute."

He stopped breathing and did a double take.

"I beg your pardon?"

"Sorry. Forward of me." She arched a brow. "Then again, nothing ventured, nothing gained."

He ran a hand down his clean-shaven jaw. Okay. This was weird. Her attitude. That openly seductive look. Where had all this come from?

"Can you tell me what day it is?"

When she sighed, closed her eyes and turned her head, he directed her face back again. As that tranquil spring-green gaze fused with his, he asked very clearly, "Do you know where you are?"

She blinked slowly and cast a glance around. "I'm in a room alone with you. Are you married?" she asked, and then smiled at herself. "There I go again. But…you aren't married, are you?" A faint line cut between her brows. "How do I know that? How do I know you?"

Daniel rocked back on his heels. *Good Lord.* "I'm Daniel. Daniel McNeal."

"Nice name. Kind of cheeky. It suits you."

She repeated his name, tasting it like a bite of warm Belgian chocolate. When her tongue held on to the final *l,* he caught himself studying her mouth, her lips, and not in a clinical way.

"How about your name?" His palm brushed her cool brow. "Know that?"

She blinked several times, screwed up her eyes tightly and thought. "I don't recall." Then she studied her surrounds more closely. "I don't remember anything."

Footfalls sounded behind them and Cara Cranshaw breezed in. When she saw Scarlet lying there with Daniel so close, she put on the brakes.

"Oops. Sorry. Didn't mean to interrupt."

Scarlet smiled across at her friend like a drunk. "Hi there."

Cara's head cocked to a sharp angle. As if she were tackling a field full of land mines, she edged forward. "Scarlet, honey, are you all right?"

"Everyone keeps asking me that." She eyeballed Daniel again. "Scarlet. Is that my name? That's a ridiculous question, isn't it? Except…you know…I feel a little confused."

Cara hurried the rest of the way. This time she spoke to Daniel. "What happened?"

"No one was out front. I heard a noise. Found her sprawled

out over there." He indicated the spot near the lace and the upended ladder.

Cara hunkered down beside her friend. "Scarlet, did you fall?"

"I don't know. I can't remember." She sent Daniel a plaintive look. "Can we go home now?"

While a rush of alarm shot up his spine, Daniel felt Cara's stunned expression gravitate from her friend across to him.

"My doctor makes house calls," she said.

"Get the front door." He was already collecting Scarlet in his arms again. "She needs a hospital."

That afternoon, a Dr. Lewis spoke to Daniel and Cara Cranshaw outside of Scarlet's private hospital room.

"Trauma to the head can sometimes cause a loss of episodic memory," Lewis said, scribbling on Scarlet's chart. "That's to say that the patient's memories of personal life experiences are impaired. Simply reminding a patient of their name and history won't trigger spontaneous recovery." He lowered the chart. "Usually memory returns of its own accord within a short time."

"Did you say *usually?*" Remembering how Scarlet had imprinted on him after waking from that fall, Daniel let the prognosis sink in. "You mean she could *stay* like this? No memory of her past, of who she is?"

From what he and Cara could determine, Scarlet had been alone when she'd tripped and knocked her head. On their way to this hospital, Scarlet had seemed confused but, thankfully, calm. Tests were performed. Other than a small contusion on the left side her head, and the fact she couldn't remember a thing, she seemed fine.

"There are instances where a patient's retrograde amnesia is permanent," the doctor went on, clipping his pen inside his white coat pocket. "It's typical that immediate events lead-ing up to the accident are permanently lost. But generally the semantic memory—a person's general knowledge about the world and her surroundings—is unaffected."

"Other than her loss of memory," Cara said, "she seems the same and yet...different."

"Give her brain time to reset after that jolt."

The doctor hadn't finished his sentence before Daniel noticed a woman trotting down the corridor. While her maroon pantsuit looked fresh from the cleaners, her demeanor was rumpled. As she stopped before them, Daniel saw she wore only one gold button earring rather than two.

Mrs. Anders nodded at Cara and ignored Daniel as she spoke to the doctor.

"I got here as soon as I could. I'm Scarlet Anders's mother. Her father's out of town, but flying back first thing." She took a breath. "I'd like to see my daughter straightaway."

The doctor filled Mrs. Anders in on her daughter's condition and concluded with "We recommend she stay in overnight for observation. Right now she wants to speak with her partner."

Mrs. Anders dabbed a white lace handkerchief against her cheek, then her brow. "Scarlet recently ended a relationship. She's confused."

"On that she was clear." The doctor nodded at Daniel. "Scarlet wants to see you."

Mrs. Anders lowered her handkerchief from her face. "But I'm her mother."

"It would help enormously," Lewis said, "if everyone remains calm and positive around her."

Mrs. Anders looked more dazed than her daughter had when Daniel had found her. "I'll tell Scarlet," he said, "that you're here."

Mrs. Anders closed her gaping mouth, then lifted her chin. "I'd appreciate that."

Daniel rapped lightly on the door before entering. Scarlet sat propped up in bed, ankles crossed, looking bored. Until she saw him. Then her expression came alive like the sky on the Fourth of July. Moving closer, he sent an encouraging smile.

"How you doing?"

"Fine. Other than the fact I can't remember who I am. It's the strangest feeling. It's like all the memories are there just waiting for a door to open but I can't quite turn the knob."

"It's only temporary."

"So they say."

But as she smiled so honestly into his eyes, something deep in Daniel's chest shifted more than a notch. Hopefully Scarlet would regain her memory, and soon, but it wasn't all bad having her look at him this way—with trust and excitement. Where a woman like Scarlet was concerned, a man could get used to this kind of attention.

"When can we go home?" she asked.

"My home's in Australia."

"Explains the accent. I thought maybe English." She shimmied back up against the pillows. "How long have we lived there?"

"You live in D.C., Scarlet. Here. You like it."

She narrowed her eyes as if trying to absorb the information. "We live ten thousand miles apart?"

"We haven't known each other long."

"And yet somehow I feel like I've known you forever."

When the light in her eyes faded, clouded by uncertainty, he reached and found her hand.

"Who knows?" he said. "Maybe we knew each other in a previous life."

"You think so?"

"Anything's possible."

Her face brightened again. "That's exactly how I feel."

Then she moved her legs, her shoulders, as if she were uncomfortable. "Can we leave now? I've had enough of tests and being cooped up."

"The doctor wants you to stay in overnight."

"But I don't have to, right?"

Still holding her slender hand in his, Daniel exhaled. That question wasn't his to field.

"Your mother's waiting outside. She wants to see you."

"My mother? Well, tell her to come in."

"You remember her?"

"Not at all. But I'd like to meet her."

A moment later, Mrs. Anders and her single earring slipped into the room. Her smile was hopeful, filled with maternal worry and love. She might be self-important but she obviously cared greatly for her daughter.

"Hello, Scarlet. How do you feel?"

Scarlet studied Mrs. Anders before disappointment dragged down her smile. "I'm sorry. I don't remember you. Not a thing."

Standing beside the bed, Mrs. Anders gave a stoic nod. "We'll show you pictures. That should help. Recent pictures. Pictures of when you were in school."

Scarlet's face pinched and her focus drifted to some imaginary spot beyond the hospital wall. "I'm not sure if it's real, whether it really happened…but I just had a thought. Some sort of a flash."

Mrs. Anders clasped her handkerchief. "Something from your old room? It's still as you left it when you moved out."

Scarlet's expression turned darker as she closed her eyes, trying to concentrate.

"It's a tire swing," she said. "And I'm playing with someone. No, it's me playing with the tire… Or I think it is."

Mrs. Anders sank into a chair. "You need to rest," she said in a thin voice. "The doctor said you should."

Scarlet's eyes opened again. She spoke softly but also firmly. "I've had enough rest. We're leaving. Daniel is taking me home."

Watching their unexpected guest peruse the penthouse's main room, Morgan wedged her hands into the back pockets of her jeans and shook her head.

"This has got to top anything you've ever gotten yourself into."

His focus on Scarlet running an appraising hand along the entertainment system, Daniel spoke out the side of his mouth. "I didn't get myself into anything. She's the one who fell."

Mrs. Anders was floored when her daughter had announced she was going home with a veritable stranger, a playboy descended from convicts. But when Scarlet stuck to her guns, the older woman had kept her cool and, cornered, Daniel had accepted her decision, too.

"I warned you, didn't I?" Morgan said in hushed tones. "Her friend showed up seconds after that accident, too. If you hadn't been there, Caroline Cranshaw would have taken her to the hospital and your Scarlet would be with her family now rather than thinking she's in love with you."

It was true. The way she looked at him, spoke to him, it was clear Scarlet was convinced they were—or should be—a couple. Which he could have handled very well two nights ago. Not so easy now.

Scarlet was checking out the DVD collection when she turned to him with an uneasy look on her face. "Any chance we can get something to eat? My stomach's growling louder than a bear come spring."

Daniel winced. Good Lord, had she really said that?

He resumed his supportive face. "Anything in particular?"

"A hamburger with extra onions would hit the spot. And

I could go for something sweet." She thought for a moment. "Jelly beans."

She blew him a big thank-you kiss and moved out onto the terrace. Through the open door, Daniel watched her eye the hanging cane seat, then hoist herself up and work it into a steady swing.

"Want that burger with a Guinness or a glass of milk?"

Daniel ignored Morgan's jibe. "Jelly beans. I saw a bowl on the table at her work. Could be the start of her memory coming back."

"In the meantime, hope you have a big stick handy. You'll need it to fight her off. Although that would spoil your fun."

"I would never take advantage of this situation."

"Believe it or not, I'm more worried that she'll take advantage of you." Morgan was headed for the door and her own suite. "I'll call to delay our flight. Then I'm off to research how bumps on the head can lead to heightened sexual urges. And, Daniel—" Morgan stopped in the opened doorway "—if you need me, call, okay?"

He surrendered a grin. "Always do."

He moved out onto the terrace. With her shoes off, Scarlet was evaluating the view from her perch on the swing.

"Your place is really nice," she said. "What did you say you do for a living?"

"I'm a geek."

"I love geeks!" Her lips swung to one side. "Or I think I do. Your secretary's nice, too."

"God, don't let her hear you call her that."

"Why?" With a certain gleam in her eye, Scarlet sat back. "Were you two an item in the past?"

"Never, ever."

Pointing out her peach-polished toes, she laughed. "Don't worry. I believe you. She likes you, but as a friend." Scarlet considered her words. "Was I always good at sizing people up?"

"You thought I was a pleasure-seeking eccentric."

"Sounds like fun."

"You didn't think so at the time."

"That woman—my mother—she's so repressed. Am I normally like that?"

He rolled back a shoulder. "Maybe a little."

"Snobby, too?"

"Let's say focused."

"Then why do you like me? You don't seem pretentious at all."

He leaned back against the solid masonry rail. "Scarlet, we're not a couple—you know that, right?"

"So you said. Still, I can't shake the feeling..." She pushed out of the swing and strolled over in her rumpled white dress. "We were involved somehow, though. I'm certain."

"*Involved* is a very strong word." He flipped a finger at her hair, cascading over one shoulder, a hypnotic river of shimmering gold. Far too distracting. Way too sexy.

"Just so you know," he said, "you like to wear your hair up."

Sweeping the waves up between her fingers, she piled the delectably tousled hair high on her head and struck an unintentionally steamy pose. "Like this?"

Daniel's mouth began to water.

"On second thought," he muttered, "leave it down."

She let go and the waves tumbled around her shoulders again. "You're okay with me being here, though, aren't you?"

"If it's going to help, sure."

"I'm already thinking a little clearer."

He sparked up. "You've remembered something?" The jelly bean connection?

"I remember this."

A teasing fingertip traced down his shirtfront. When her nail reached his belt buckle, every one of his reflexes jumped and, like a sprung trap, his hand caught hers. This was getting out of control, and it wasn't just her. His autonomic nervous system needed a stern talking-to.

"Believe me," he said in a thick voice, "that's not a good idea."

She didn't listen. Only smiled, then craned up on tiptoe to drag her lips down the left side of his neck. She hummed in her throat.

"I knew you'd taste like that," she murmured. "And I'm getting another flash."

Calling on willpower reserves, he put his hands on her shoulders and gently, calmly, held her back. "I don't think you should tell me."

"You have a mole under your left nipple. Am I right?"

"Wrong."

"A scar on your right thigh?"

"Nope."

"I'm sure I could find one if I looked hard enough."

As he gazed down into those bewitching green eyes, he felt his focus sharpen. Her lips were parted. Glistening. Pitilessly tempting.

Down low and deep inside where a man knows no conscience, he felt a telltale tug. Okay. More a cosmic push. He'd never wanted to kiss any woman more than he wanted to kiss Scarlet Anders right now. Mindlessly, relentlessly and well into the coming night.

But he'd told Morgan. Warned himself. It wasn't happening. Not when Scarlet didn't know her own mind.

With his hands still cupping her shoulders, he had every intention of shifting her to one side, stepping out of harm's way. Instead, he was aware of fingers curling over her upper back at the same time her palms traveled up his chest to each side of his neck. The impulse to react in an unmistakably positive way filled his veins with so much molten want, a sweat broke on his brow.

Worse, while his hands brought her closer, his head angled down. Her mouth was an undeniable hairbreadth away and his inner caveman wouldn't quit grunting. *Do it. Do it.* An educated, just as unhelpful voice assured him that he was doing the right thing. *Acting on reproductive chemistry is the natural order of things. Good God, man, what are you waiting for?*

Hell, she was practically begging.

Gritting his teeth, cursing both sides of his nature, he maneuvered until she was a good arm's length away.

"We need to stop."

"I know we've done this before. We've kissed." One slender shoulder lifted and dropped. "Might help my memory if we did it again."

She edged forward but, digging painfully deep, he stood his ground.

"If you keep this up, you'll go home to your parents."

Her eyebrows hitched. "You can't talk to me like that. I'm an adult."

"Then act like one."

She opened her mouth, ready to object. But then her peeved expression eased. With a vaguely apologetic air, she sauntered inside while Daniel was left to slump against the balcony rail. He wanted to deflect trouble but, Lord in heaven, he also wanted to embrace it. And he had the biggest feeling this changed Scarlet knew that as well as he did.

So how long did she expect to stay here and torture him? How long before he caved in?

Six

Scarlet snuggled back on the enormous black leather sofa.

"I'm still sighing over the hamburger." She eyed her generous host, Daniel McNeal, who was slotting a DVD into his kick-ass entertainment center's player. "You seriously missed out."

"My steak was good. I'm completely satisfied."

As he glanced over, Scarlet soaked up the entrancing slant of his grin. She might have lost her memory but anyone could spot a heartthrob when she saw one. From the moment she'd laid eyes on the man who had come to her rescue when she'd apparently fallen and knocked her poor head, she'd been smitten. Frankly, love-struck. He might insist they weren't "together," but the way she caught him sometimes looking at her, with that need-to-have-you gleam in his eye, she'd put her money on intuition. He was dying to kiss her, to hold her tight. As much as she wanted to kiss and hold him right back.

A bowl of candy sat between her legs. "Want a jelly bean?" she asked, chewing.

"I'm not a sweet tooth."

Digging around, she picked out two more. "I'm really liking the pink ones."

As he lowered down beside her, she lobbed one up into the air. With a click against her teeth, it landed in her mouth. Encouraged—she must have done this before—she tried again. This one bounced off her nose. On reflex, Daniel caught the bean a heartbeat before it landed in her lap. Continuing the motion, his hand skimmed her leg before he dropped the bean back in her opened palm.

She studied his profile as he continued to fiddle with volume and selections. He wanted her to believe that he was unaffected. But, accident or not, the back of his hand had grazed her bare thigh. The sensation had sent every one of her arousal receptors firing and beeping on high. How were his hot points holding up?

"Thanks for letting me use your shower," she said as the movie's opening credits appeared. "And lending me the clothes."

Setting the remote aside, he flicked over a glance. "The shirt is way oversized." Feeling safe and warm, Scarlet hugged herself. *I don't mind.* "Tomorrow we'll bring some of your gear over."

"I can stay?"

"I'm hoping your memory will show up soon."

"I don't know." She settled back. "I think it might be enjoying the break. All those obligations I have at that DC Affairs place. I'm a partner in the biggest, most successful party-planning company in the city?"

"From all accounts, you love what you do."

"That woman, Cara, told me about a huge cathedral wedding I'm supposed to be organizing." She held her head. "Talk about brain overload. I'd rather relax and watch *Spider-Man*."

The lights in Daniel's eyes blinked on. "That's right."

"What's right?"

"You're a *Spider-Man* fan."

Scarlet thought about it. Well…yeah. Sure. She liked *Spider-Man*. Didn't everyone?

"What else do you remember?" he asked.

"You mean, other than the way I feel about you?"

"We've been through that."

"Not really. Not the history." She settled in more. "What happened between the two of us?"

"You said 'no' on more than one occasion."

"That doesn't gel with how I feel now."

"You're not well."

He let her take his hand. She laid his palm on her brow, her cheek. She nodded solemnly. "Guess I am feeling a little warm."

He took his hand away. "This isn't a joke."

"I thought you had a sense of humor."

"Not where this is concerned."

She shimmied down into her seat. "Fine. Then we'll sit here and quietly watch the movie. Got any popcorn?"

"Does butter have two *t*'s?"

A few moments later he returned with a freshly popped bowl. When he set it between them, she scooped out a handful. Her first taste was soft and light and brilliantly salty. She filled her mouth again and tried to fix her attention on the movie's opening scene. But the story sitting beside her in a bad-boy white tee was a thousand times more intriguing.

"Tell me more about Daniel McNeal," she said between chews.

"I'm an Australian IT guy who got lucky and made a fortune putting together a social media site."

"I want to know about *you,* Daniel. Who you are inside." She set the jelly bean bowl aside and, bringing up her legs, hugged her knees while she faced him and nibbled more popcorn. "Tell me about growing up in Australia."

"That was a long time ago."

"It might help spur on some of my own memories."

He closed one eye, then shrugged. "I lived in the western suburbs of Sydney. Working-class. Public schools."

"And not near the sea."

"I'm making up for that now."

He told her about a big yacht he moored at a place called Port Hinchinbrook and a small cog clicked into place. She remembered…something. But she didn't let on. When it came to talking about himself, Daniel was as tight as a rusted faucet. Now he'd started, she didn't want to stop the flow.

"What did your parents do for a living?" she asked.

"My mother stayed at home."

"Baking apple pies?"

"Scones. Great warm, with mountains of jam and loads of butter."

"I wonder if I can cook."

"If you can't, that makes two of us."

Smiling, she scooped out more popcorn. "Where is she now?"

"My mother died when I was young. I told you that."

He hadn't told this Scarlet. "I'm sorry," she said softly. "What about your father? What's he like?"

"He's dead, too."

"When you were young?" He nodded. "Do you remember what he was like?"

"I remember he worked a lot. He was a carpenter."

"A noble trade. Did he play ball with you on weekends? Take you fishing?"

"He worked."

"He must have had a day off."

"No, he didn't." His gaze dropped. "Not until he absolutely had to."

She apologized again. "I didn't mean to make you sad."

He looked at her as if her hair had turned bright green. "I'm not sad. I'm…nothing." He glared at the TV screen. "Let's forget it."

Scarlet filled her mouth with popcorn. She'd pushed enough. His face was suddenly so hard. His body so still. Whatever had happened between Daniel and his dad ran deep and still cut. Which begged the question: Did she have a dark moment in her past? Something she'd sooner forget?

She pushed the popcorn bowl away. Suddenly she was full. A better word was *stuffed.*

"I've had enough."

"For a lightweight," he said, "you sure can pack away the tucker."

"Is that an Aussie term for food?" When he nodded, she flopped onto her side. "Well, don't feed me any more tucker tonight. If I don't like exercise, I'm in trouble with the scales."

"How's your head?"

"No pain. Though I still feel a little odd." She found the right word. "Separate." Apart.

When she'd been in the hospital, that woman—her mother—had unsettled her. Thinking of Faith Anders even now sent a shiver scuttling over her skin. But she couldn't pinpoint why.

"I didn't want to go home with that woman," she admitted.

"She's your mother."

"With every bone in my body, it doesn't feel that way."

"Maybe because you'd already made up your mind about staying with me."

"I know you think I'm playing games, but I'm not. I feel safe with you."

His smile was wry. "If only the 'old you' could hear that."

"I can't say why I acted or thought the way I did before today. I can only tell you how it feels to be me now."

"You're entitled to feel any way you want."

"Do you mean that?"

"Even though I'm aware it's a trick question."

"So would it be entirely wrong for you to put your arm around me now? You know, just to give me an idea of whether I'm actually off course."

"Perhaps you need to ask your father if that's a good idea."

She scowled. Her father?

"I'm an adult," she said. "If you don't like me the way I am now, well, I suppose that's another story."

"You're trying to manipulate me."

"Oh, but you're too smart for that."

Then she went ahead and did what she knew they both wanted her to do. She sidled up, reached back and wrapped his arm around her. Wanting to sigh at the warmth and the strength in his touch, she snuggled against his chest.

"There. See? That's not so bad." As she fit the sash of his arm more securely around her, she thought she might have felt the scuff of his chin brush her crown.

"I can see two things happening down the track," he said. "You abusing me for taking advantage of this situation—"

"Or us falling in love again."

"Again? We were never in love."

She grazed her lips over his upper arm. "Are you sure?" She grazed again. Dropped a light kiss.

She felt his chest harden against her.

"Define *love,*" he said.

"It's an overwhelming emotion that starts like a spark at your core. Then as you grow closer, that flicker gets brighter, warmer, until it's a flame licking through every channel of your body, heating every part of you inside and out. It's like being put in the perfect toaster and getting more and more ready to pop."

"You feel that way now?"

"I feel as if those flames are building. Like I want them to consume me, scorch and singe me. I want that burn to go on forever. At the same time I need to have that blaze put out."

"Let me guess how."

He had a smile in his voice. She smiled, too. Then with deliberate care she shifted and began to unbutton her shirt. She didn't think he quite knew what was happening…until she let one side fall open. As the air met her flesh, he stiffened. But he didn't pull back.

Feeling she'd done this before, she moved one leg just enough for the shirttails to fall more apart. Reaching, she found his hand and guided his palm over her ribs, past her navel until his fingertips feathered the naked mound between her legs. If she didn't think he'd been here before, she might feel shy.

His fingers curled and drew away. "You planned this?"

"I didn't have any fresh underwear, is all."

She heard the amused smile in his voice. "Scarlet, you're just plain wicked."

She pressed against him. "I can be much more than that."

He probably should have thought it through. What would happen if he buckled? How would he justify taking advantage of her this way—to himself, to her family or to Scarlet when she was more herself? She might be pushing hard but he was in control of this situation.

Or he ought to be.

None of those arguments were worth a damn when she craned higher and their lips just seemed to fit together. And as their mouths fused and locked and they each began to explore with hands, with tongues, any reasoning about regrets flew from his head like dust on a windy day. On one important point, Scarlet had it right. They may have kissed only once before tonight but they had indeed shared some smoldering moments. As his palm sculpted her side and brought her irrevocably near, he accepted their fate. Right or wrong, weak or strong, he would have her in his bed tonight.

With his mouth covering hers, he was acutely aware of her open shirt, of her breasts—and every blessed part of her from there on down. With her soft warm flesh held tight against him, he savored the magnified buzz in his groin and steady throb of his blood as he responded to every one of her positive signals. With persuasive fingers filing up through his hair and a naked thigh winding over his lap, multiple ideas of how he might be able to please her unwound in his mind like an endless yarn.

His palm traced up her side again before, thumb winging out, he caught and measured the weight of her breast. Then he angled his thumb higher, teasing a nipple until its peak was hard and she was pushing against him.

Her lips on his, she whispered, "I knew it would feel like this." That was followed by an echoing beat in time, then a jolt of conscience. But to his bones he believed the woman burning for his affections now was the real, less inhibited Scarlet Anders. That fall had been an accident, but the way she was kissing him, pressing up against him, making sweet moaning noises deep in her throat…

This was no mistake.

She shifted her thigh until she was perched spread-eagled on his lap. Like the answer to a dream, her two exquisite breasts appeared before his eyes. Lower, courtesy of the plasma's flickering light, he admired a flat tummy and, a hand span below her navel, that open invitation. When she arched toward him, his mouth found the tip of her breast at the same time he whipped her over and on her back.

His right knee nudged between her legs as his left foot planted on the floor to balance his weight. While her feathery touch rode the slopes from his neck to his shoulders, he gently sucked, lightly nipped, before swapping to worship her other breast. One long silken leg coiled up over the back of his thigh. The calf grazed his side several times as if judging the best place to land. When he nipped a little harder, she writhed and her leg clamped down.

Straightening, he grabbed the hem of his T-shirt and ripped the white interlock up and over his head. He was about to tackle his jeans when his gaze found hers. Her eyes appeared both slumberous and hungry, the look of a lioness after the kill, enjoying the start of her meal. She could feast on him as long as she pleased. Still...

Here tonight, under such unusual circumstances, he had to ask again.

His hands settling on either side of her head, he leaned in and said, "You're sure this is what you want?"

She laughed softly, a throaty sexy sound. Moving beneath him like a sleek and restless cat, she found his hand and ran his palm down the line of her throat, between her breasts, over her tummy and lower. When his touch slid between her soft folds, urgent heat flashed through his veins. She was slick and warm. Unmistakably ready.

With his gaze locked on hers, his fingers rode back up to find that sensitive nub. Her breath hitched, eyes shut and pelvis lifted to meet him, and he began to circle and rub oh-so-lightly. Her hips started to move, too, small irregular rotations, while a contented smile hooked the corners of her mouth. After a few moments, when she'd coiled her arms over her head and looked as if she might take off, he moved to ditch his jeans.

Joining her again, she reached for him. While her hands roamed up and down the length of his arms, he returned to his labor of love, concentrating on pleasing her, gauging her reactions to various methods, working out what she liked best. When he sensed that the tension running through her had built to a critical pushing-the-ceiling point, he positioned himself and nudged the head of his erection inside of her.

The sensation was a fierce visceral rush that flashed hot from that point of his anatomy to every cell in his body. Air brushed the damp skin between his shoulder blades as he throbbed and hardened more. Then he became vaguely aware of something flat and small resting below his throat where his heart was threatening to Olympic broad jump out of his chest. A hand was pressing him away.

She wanted him to stop?

Now?

"What's wrong?" he ground out.

"You forgot something."

He tried to think what.

"Daniel, we want to be safe."

Drawing back, he swore to himself. Guess there was a first time for everything. Still, he couldn't believe he'd been so careless about something so important. Something that could have repercussions for the rest of their lives. He for one was not ready for parenthood. Sometimes he wondered if he ever would be.

He pushed up onto bare feet.

"I'll be back."

She was already curling up off the longue. "You're not going anywhere without me."

Standing before him, she wound her arms around his middle as her lips traced a teasing line over his chest, up under his throat to his chin. His head at an angle, he nibbled the fragrant side of her neck while his hands rounded over the rise of her buns. When she stretched on tiptoe and wiggled, he held her firm and bent at his knees. He wanted to be closer, needed to be joined. He longed to thrust up inside of her again, this time all the way.

Releasing the hold on her backside, he grabbed the opening of her shirt. After peeling the fabric from her back, he tossed the shirt aside, then hoisted her up off her feet. As her legs snap-locked around his hips and her arms looped about his neck, his mouth captured hers again. Only this time, there was no holding back. This kiss was reckless. Desperate.

On autopilot, he headed for the main bedroom. Not because they needed the convention of a mattress. He'd have consummated this next step on a hessian bag in the middle of the Gobi Desert if that was the offer. His mission was to find the packet in his bedside drawer, and find it fast, because it was getting near impossible to keep his mind on being responsible. With every step, their caresses grew wilder, the fire flared brighter. She was deliberately sliding up and down against him like that, teasing him shamelessly. And he loved her for it.

In the bedroom, he balanced her with one arm and whipped back the covers with the other. Then he dropped her on the sheet among the pillows and threw open the dresser drawer. After sheathing himself, he joined her, prowling up and over her legs, tasting a line of creamy smooth flesh along the way. When they were eye to eye again, she tilted her head in a pretty pose, reached down and gripped him tight in a fist. Daniel jerked at the bolt of pleasure before growing very still.

She dragged her hand up, squeezed back down, then pumped him a few more breathtaking times. He was spellbound, hovering between sublime pleasure and can't-hold-on-much-longer bliss. By the time she released him, her message was clear.

We can't get more ready than this.

Drawing her knees back toward her hips, he settled between her opened thighs. Then he eased inside enough to have her catch a quick breath, adjust and melt into the sheet. Her lips were parted, glistening and so tempting. One of her arms was looped over her head. His hand circled her wrist before he plunged and entered her fully. While his nerve endings jumped and quivered, her hand flexed and she arched up.

"I remember..." she murmured, and everything, including Daniel's heart, seemed to stop.

Remembered? How much? Enough to know how determined she'd been in a previous life that this shouldn't happen? Enough for her to jerk away and slap his face before storming out, fuming? Possibly crying?

"I remember," she said, drawing a line around the curve of his jaw with her free hand, "feeling this way. Being with you...like this."

Daniel let out a breath. He half wanted to correct her, tell her she was wrong. That this was the first incredible time. But he decided he'd let her believe what she liked, at least for now.

As his lips trailed across her brow, his hips moved again in a regular controlled rhythm, but as the burn of pleasure turned from scorching to white-hot, his momentum increased. She was moving, too, her efforts to meet him coming faster and stronger, until his climax was a pulsating heartbeat away. Then the walls began to shake and that amazing heat evolved into an almighty blazing pressure. When her hips kicked up to join his, Daniel's mouth crashed down on hers again.

As they both climaxed, he couldn't imagine a time when he would ever want this to end.

Wicked?

Where sex was concerned, Scarlet could teach the devil to dance.

Scarlet basked in the afterglow of her orgasm-like-no-other. His long strong body steaming above hers, Daniel seemed just as spent. Just as satisfied. Was it any wonder that, after making love with this incredible man, she felt not only uniquely uplifted but also was craving more?

Although she couldn't remember their relationship before today, in her heart she not only knew Daniel McNeal, she cared for him a great deal. Whenever she took in his ruggedly handsome face, that mischievous lopsided smile, instinct said that being together this way was, perhaps, the most beautiful experience of her life. These past few moments spent in his arms—being the lucky recipient of all that sizzling sexual prowess—felt as true to her as the divine order of the universe.

Pretty big statement.

Had she always viewed romantic love in such cosmic terms? Had securing this depth of belonging always been a priority? Tonight she felt as if she'd snatched a taste of the ultimate treasure. The only real essential in this life.

But deeper, in a shadowy place, she also felt off balance— somehow on edge—as if a well-hidden part of her was braced, waiting for some random shoe to drop.

A contented growl rumbled through Daniel's sternum before, with a final meaning-filled kiss, he rolled off to her side. When his arm slipped beneath her shoulders, Scarlet promptly cuddled in. The corners of her mouth curved up and sleepy eyes drifted shut. That odd shoe-waiting-to-drop feeling faded completely away.

"How are you feeling?"

Scarlet's hum was dreamy. "*Terrible*. Talk about a disappointment."

His arm stiffened before he shifted to gauge her expression. Then, in the misted light slanting in through the terrace doors, the corners of his eyes crinkled and he settled down again. Soon, hot fingertips began to trail up and down her arm. Drifting along on this cozy lull, she wondered if she could read his mind.

"You're thinking what happens next," she said.

"I know what I'd like to have happen."

"Me, too."

Recovered enough, she moved to swing herself up and over him. Chuckling, he held her back in place.

"Hey, slow down, cowgirl."

"We had sex." Brilliant, blistering, must-have-more sex. Her kiss-swollen lips drew a playful ring around his closest nipple. "No reason it shouldn't happen again."

"That's a self-serving argument."

"Mutually self-serving."

They'd only licked the surface.

Her mouth trailed higher. When she reached the beating hollow below his Adam's apple, she twirled her tongue around the dip while her hand snaked down over the steely bumps of his six-pack and lower. His hand caught hers.

Relenting, she exhaled. "I want you, Daniel. There's nothing sinister or sick in that."

"You don't *know* me."

Sitting up, she purposely neglected covering herself with the sheet. She liked being naked with Daniel. She couldn't get naked enough, and she *knew* now he felt the same way.

"I know everything I need to know," she said, but he only looked off. Her lips pressed together. "Why is that so hard for you to accept? You were as keen as I was to get that first time out of the way."

He stared at her. "Our *first* time?"

Frowning, she rubbed her temple. If they hadn't been intimate together until now, why did she feel as if they'd been lovers since time had begun? Rounds of recognition fired through her system whenever she looked at him, whenever they touched. That wasn't imagination. That was previous experience.

Wasn't it?

Behind her, he propped himself up on one elbow and the rough of his chin began to draw leisurely patterns low on her back. Then his lips dragged over the same primed spots. As her senses responded—scent, touch, smell, popping to life again—she closed her eyes and concentrated on the drugging sensations such simple acts could create. She wanted him to kiss her all over like that...on every fingertip, across her brow, along the sweep between hip and quivering thigh.

She wanted that magic to spill stardust over every parched inch of her. Damn it, she ached to unlock the mystery that made this man so good.

"Scarlet, I'm saying we need to be careful."

"I thought you were the laid-back type?"

He stopped. "How do you know I'm laid-back?"

Scarlet froze, too, and, as a cool damp broke on her forehead, tried to think. How *had* she known?

Well...because...she just did. And she didn't like the way he was dissecting everything she said. Making her doubt intuition when that was pretty much all she had to go on. She got that he was trying to help her recover her memory but didn't that include finding out how they fit? She needed to know about Daniel McNeal.

"You didn't answer my question," she said.

Was he laid-back? A lock-up-your-daughters type?

His response was to swing his legs out of bed and head for the attached bath. Scarlet eased out of bed, too. She was tempted to stroll around without clothes...although she didn't think she was an exhibitionist; she wouldn't parade about without a stitch in front of just anyone. And if he wanted to know, she just *knew* that, too. But while Daniel had obviously enjoyed making love tonight, he was torn over the fact he might have taken advantage of her, which he had not. She'd given her consent. More than once.

Still, she didn't want to stir his pot too much.

She looked around. Not a stray shirt or robe anywhere to be seen. She could sneak a peek inside his wardrobe, she supposed. But he might take that as snooping. Instead, she tugged the top bedsheet out and wrapped herself up, toga style. Then she crossed to the bureau and squinted to see in the misty light.

Typical of a bachelor. Nothing personal in the way of photos or knickknacks. Nothing that would give a glimpse of insight into his life, his history.

Apparently she had her own town house in Georgetown. At the hospital, before saying goodbye, that lovely Cara woman had offered to stay there with her, but she'd insisted on coming home with Daniel. Now, however, she felt a niggling to see her own place. How did she like to decorate? What photos, memories, would she find on the shelves and mantel? What clues would she discover about either liking her life or wanting to bag it?

The click of a door opening echoed through the room. Still gloriously naked, Daniel ambled out of the bathroom. In silvery ribbons of light, he stood feet apart, thighs locked, big shoulders back. Scarlet shivered at the pull of their instant connection, the intense urge to have him hold her again. While his eyes glittered across at her, both his hands flexed at his sides. He studied the toga—and released a grin.

"I'm underdressed."

She pulled the sheet away and let it drop to her toes. "My mistake."

His gaze sharpened in a flattering way and, at once, she felt uplifted. She felt…adored. And perhaps that was an accelerated, hormone-induced state but, regardless, as she'd explained earlier, a person couldn't control her emotions. And just as she felt this connection, the bond that said she belonged with him, she also believed he felt that connection, too.

After a nerve-racking moment, he sauntered forward.

When he stopped before her, he studied her lips, the slope of her neck. Drawing herself up, she waited again for the hypnotic lure of his touch.

His gaze locked with hers. Then his foot kicked out, the sheet flew up and he caught a handful before shaking out the rest. He thrust the bundle forward.

"Put this on," he said. "You'll catch cold."

Her heart sank. Then she took the damn sheet. And dropped it over *his* shoulder.

"I think you're the one who's into covering up."

"I'm not trying to cover up anything." He put an arm out, spun her and, with the motion, the sheet wound around and draped her again.

"Then why won't you answer my question?" she asked, a little giddy. "Talk to me."

"It's your memory we want to jog, not mine."

Her grin was wry. He sure was a tough one to crack.

Moving to the bed, she sat on its lower end. "Do you really want me to stay with that woman?"

"You mean your mother?" He found a pair of gym shorts slung over the back of a corner chair, which was hidden by shadows. "Thing is, I'd planned to fly back to Australia today."

While he stepped into the shorts, her chest tightened. Her accident had kept him here? How had yesterday's Scarlet felt about him leaving?

"Guess you have important stuff to get back to?" she asked.

"It's just time I left."

"You'll visit your house in that Hinchinbrook place?"

"And go out on my yacht every day for a week. Probably anchor down overnight somewhere far away from it all."

"I might not remember my own life but I know D.C. is hardly away from it all."

"Kinda my point."

"What else will you do?"

"Go for a good long ride on my bike. Lie on a beach. Catch up with friends."

"And family?"

He hesitated. "Sure. Family, too."

"Then you should go. Go tomorrow. First thing."

Clearly unconvinced, he rubbed his linebacker chest. "Where would that leave you?"

"Everyone says I'll have my memory back soon. Probably a couple of days. I'll stay with Faith Anders."

"Your father's home tomorrow."

Her skin prickled and she shuddered. None of that mother/ father stuff felt right. Being there alone with an older couple she didn't know, she'd feel like the only kid at a party without a friend. Awkward.

She dragged the sheet higher toward her throat.

"Maybe I'll hang around at DC Affairs. Try to help."

"You heard Cara. She's been in touch with your other partner," he said. "She and Ariella are more than capable of holding down the fort while you recuperate."

She drew lines in the carpet with her toes. "I suppose I wouldn't be much use. But I have all this time on my hands. I could have a great vacation, if I only knew what I liked to do. Where I'd want to go."

"You once said you wanted to see Australia."

She focused on him and a word flashed into her mind. "Kangaroos." She surrendered a small smile. "Sorry. That just popped into my head. I wasn't throwing out the world's biggest hint." She added, "And I know there's a whole lot more to your country than those cute fluffy things."

He rubbed his jaw. "You really need to see a full-grown red in person." He wandered over to the bed and sat beside her. "Australia's big and brassy and, yes, amazingly beautiful."

She looked him up and down. "Figures."

He was all that and more. But as much as she wanted to be with him—share more of this—she'd held him up enough. When she got her memory back, she might try to pin him down again.

Getting to her feet, she hooked a thumb toward the living room. "I might go veg out there for the night."

He glanced at the bed before his gaze lowered and he said, "There are spare bedrooms."

"Thanks, but I think I'll curl up on the couch and rewind that DVD."

He nodded slowly, then shrugged. "Want some company?"

"I'd rather watch it on my own, if that's okay." She headed out. "Get a good night's rest."

She heard the humorless smile in his voice. "You make it sound like I was the one who spent the afternoon in the hospital."

She stopped at the doorway. "I'll be gone in the morning." She gave a weak smile. "'Thanks for everything' sounds so twee. But…you know what I mean."

She walked out of the room feeling his eyes burning two holes in her back and hearing a rendition of doubt going around in her head. Maybe she ought to feel embarrassed, ashamed, by the way she'd come on to him tonight. Hell, maybe when she remembered who she was, she'd be disappointed in herself.

But for the life of her, this minute she couldn't summon a morsel of regret. She only knew she didn't have the right to put Daniel through this mental tug-of-war.

After slipping on her discarded shirt, she rebooted the DVD, settled on the couch and tried to imagine how it would feel to have all her memories back. In some ways that was scarier than the void she lived with now. The far more frightening question was…

What if she never remembered her past?

Seven

Yawning, Scarlet dragged her sleepy gaze around the room. A big plasma screen, a popcorn-strewn coffee table, a soft blanket lain across her chest. She blinked several times. Where the hell was she?

A familiar deep voice drifted down to her.

"You looked so comfortable I didn't want to wake you."

With a start, Scarlet sat up. A man. Daniel McNeal. She remembered him taking her to the hospital, automatically felt for the bump on her head. Yes, it was still there.

"I remember."

His chin went up. "Everything?"

"Only yesterday, after the accident." When he nodded, her attention dropped to his lips, then to his shoulders and chest, encased this morning in a casual button-down. The cuffs were folded back to below each elbow. She focused on his big tan hands and a frisson of awareness ripped through her.

She sat back. "And I remember last night."

With a crooked grin, he rubbed the back of his neck. "Not easy to forget."

"I don't regret it," she said quickly, to set him at ease if his conscience was bothering him.

"Me, either."

He put out a hand and she accepted his tug up. Setting aside how warm and strong his fingers felt wrapped around hers—how nice it would have been to have spent last night in his bed—she peered through the sliding-glass doors to the drizzly day outside.

"What time is it?" she asked.

"Time we got moving."

"Places to go," she reminded herself.

That went for both of them.

"I'll call Cara," she said as he brought two full coffee mugs from the dining room table and set one next to the popcorn bowl. "She won't mind taking me to Faith Anders's house."

"I'm taking you."

"You've put up with enough." Inhaling the rich, just-perked aroma, she warmed her hands around the mug. "I won't put you out anymore."

Before falling asleep last night, she'd cemented her decision. On one hand they were incredibly physically compatible; last night proved that when they got together, they were as combustible as a tinderbox. On the other he was reluctant to get involved any deeper on that level. He was adamant she wouldn't feel anywhere near as chummy toward him when her memory returned. Because of something he wasn't telling her? Maybe if she spent time with Cara and her parents she'd find out more. Then again her memory might return tomorrow and all would be revealed.

"You haven't put me out," he assured her, taking a long pull from his mug.

"You're flying home today. You need to take care of that. Simple."

"Wrong. It's incredibly complicated. Your mother entrusted your well-being to me. I'm responsible for delivering you back into your parents' charge."

She set down her cup. "I don't like being treated like a child who needs to be dropped off at day care."

"Tough."

A smile touched one corner of her mouth. "You're way too alpha to be a true geek."

"Not according to the pack of wolves that raised me." He'd crossed back to the dining table to collect a pile of clothes. As she joined him, he handed the stash over to her.

"Morgan's loaned you some casual wear," he added, "including underwear."

"Because you mentioned I didn't wear any panties last night?"

"I didn't mention it. She guessed."

Scarlet took the clothes. Holding the khaki pants and orange grunge print tee against herself, she pondered. "Those white patent sling-backs are gonna clash big-time."

"Morgan also supplied a selection of footwear comprising purple flip-flops and boots that look like they were previously modeled by Minnie Mouse."

Thirty minutes later, they'd finished enjoying a monster strawberry pancake breakfast that had arrived at the door housed beneath shiny silver domes. Between mouthfuls of coffee, Daniel phoned Cara to get the Anderses' address and, after she'd assembled her few belongings, they were nestled once again in his dynamite car. Revving out of the undercover parking space into a steady mist of rain, Scarlet wiggled her toes in her Minnie Mouse shoes.

"My parents won't recognize me, will they?"

"Clothes do not a woman make." He slid her a playful smile. "Besides, eclectic works for you."

She struck a hip-hop pose from the waist up. "I have an urge to dive into a dead cockroach spin."

The cabin filled with the sound of his laughter, so deep and sexy Scarlet didn't want to think about saying goodbye to it. Saying goodbye to *him*.

"Hate to break it to you," he said, "but you're a huge classical fan."

A memory clicked and a distant tinkling echoed up from a deep funnel in her brain. The haunting strains of music followed. Then the noise of the rain hitting the windscreen and the swish of wipers faded in. Coming back to the here and now, she glanced across at Daniel. His attention was fixed on the wet road and traffic. Probably best not to tell him about that trickle of insight, she decided, planting her shoes in the foot well. No use getting him or anyone else excited.

Soon Daniel was pulling up to her parents' Georgetown address and parking the Italian sports car at twelve on the semicircular drive. As he opened Scarlet's door, she alighted having formed the opinion that the Anderses' home was more a manicured mansion. Neoclassical in style, it featured giant columns, a large pediment, full-length porch and symmetrical facade.

And how did she know all that terminology? she wondered, walking alongside Daniel up the broad porch steps. Perhaps she'd knocked over some architectural courses in college. Not that she could remember being part of a sorority or anything.

Faith Anders answered the door. Scarlet tried her best to spark a memory but nothing about the woman's silvery-blond hairdo or cosmetically enhanced lips was familiar. However, when Faith lifted her chin as she took in her daughter's ensemble, Scarlet felt a twinge. Not pleasant.

Gathering herself, Faith extended both arms for a hug.

Scarlet did what was polite and stepped into the embrace. As her mother's cool fingers curled around her, remarkably she felt some warmth—a faint click—but nothing to shout about. At least she didn't feel quite so reluctant to step inside now.

"Your father's home," Faith said, looking both uneasy and relieved.

"Hope I didn't worry him too much," Scarlet replied, entering the sparkling foyer ahead of Daniel.

"He's eager to see you." Then she turned to Daniel and spoke down her nose at him, no mean feat given he was a head and a half taller. "Thank you for looking after her last night."

"It was my pleasure," he replied solemnly.

Scarlet flicked him a look. So cool. *You are a bad boy.*

They followed Faith into a house decked out with miles of oak-paneled walls, sumptuous window dressings and museum-quality art. Taking her time, Scarlet ran her fingertips along surfaces and objects as they moved through the hall and came to a large, immaculately decorated room. The smooth, mirror-polished entry table adorned with a bowl of perfumed roses...the gilded frame of a Renaissance painting depicting a preoccupied-looking woman holding a toddler... the curve of a gleaming baby grand piano.

Score on the memory gauge?

Zip.

Near the unlit fireplace, a man in his sixties reclined in a wingback chair. On seeing them arrive, he pushed to his feet and straightened the hem of his smoking jacket. So people really wore those things? Scarlet wondered.

"Sweetheart," he said, and put out his arms as Faith had done a minute earlier. But again there wasn't an inkling of recognition. Worse, she realized she didn't know her own father's name. As go-with-the-flow as she'd been yesterday, she felt more and more puzzled today.

She moved forward and allowed the man to bring her close,

rub her back. That was when she noticed Cara Cranshaw standing nearby, waiting patiently. Now, smiling, her friend nodded hello.

"Scarlet," Cara said. "You look so rested."

"Although no one would recognize her in those clothes," her mother said, indicating with a gesture that everyone should sit as she lowered into a chair that matched her husband's. Scarlet took a seat on the embroidered couch.

"I haven't seen your curls that wild since—" Faith seemed to catch herself before straightening the cuffs of her gray silk blouse. "You're usually a fanatic with your hair. I remember when you were six and wanted to cut every recalcitrant strand off."

Scarlet caught her hair in a ponytail and flicked it onto her back. "There's a lot of it."

Tipping forward, her father tapped one of several photo albums set out on the mahogany coffee table. "Your mother let me know what the doctor said—that your memory will return of its own accord. But no harm in taking a walk down memory lane."

Daniel had remained standing. Now Cara moved across to join her friend on the couch. Scarlet picked up an album and murmured, "Thanks...Dad."

She felt odd calling a man she saw as a stranger by that name.

She opened the album to the first page and saw a picture of herself looking like a red-carpet invitee in a black silk cocktail dress, raising a champagne flute and beaming along with a room full of equally jubilant people.

"That's the official opening of DC Affairs." Cara pointed out another photo of Scarlet with her arm around a stunning-looking woman. "That's Ariella, your partner."

Scarlet ran a fingertip around the photo. "When can I meet her?"

"I rang to tell her we were gathering here this morning," Cara said. "She wanted to be here but…" Her friend's expression wavered. "Ariella has a few things going on. She was in the middle of setting up a very important meeting."

Something I would have known about yesterday, no doubt.

"You'd have all these photos downloaded somewhere," her father said.

"You printed these out just for us," Faith added.

Scarlet set aside the album. She wanted something older. One that was covered in cartoon ponies drew her eye. Inside, photos showed a girl with fiery red-gold hair lashed down in plaits at a ballet recital, then blowing candles out on a cake and, finally, sitting at a piano, tiny fingers on keys.

Her stomach filled with butterflies. This was weird.

She tapped the last photo. "Here I am playing chopsticks."

Faith Anders stiffened. "Never that. Even at that age we knew you had talent."

"Your mother plays, too," her father said.

Scarlet took that in. Earlier Daniel had mentioned she liked classical music. "So I got my taste and talent from you?"

Faith's eyelids flickered and she eased into a smile. "I won't take credit. You were always destined to be a far better player than me."

Scarlet slid the album back onto the table. "Maybe when I see my old room…"

But suddenly her brain hurt. She felt drained. When she pressed her hand against her temple—it was as if someone were winding a diamond-tipped screw in there—Cara touched her shoulder.

"Do you need to rest?" her friend asked. "Lie down?"

"I shouldn't need to. I slept like the dead last night."

Faith visibly shuddered. "Scarlet, please don't say those kinds of things."

It was on the tip of Scarlet's tongue to point out that it was just an expression but that would have been rude. And something told her, if anything, she wasn't that.

"I even nodded off before I got to the end of the latest *Spider-Man* DVD," she said instead.

Faith laughed delicately. "But you've never been into superheroes."

"Perhaps she never mentioned it to you," Cara pointed out.

Faith sat back. "I can't see why not."

"Point is," her father said, "you're home now. We'll work it out."

Scarlet rapped her shoes' toes on the million-dollar carpet. *Home...* That wasn't here. And it wasn't with Daniel. Right now, she didn't know where she belonged.

Out of nowhere, the back of her nose began to prickle and moisture filled her eyes. But she willed the emotion away. This topsy-turvy state wouldn't last forever. She'd had glimpses of her previous life. Soon, as the doctor had said, everything would fall into place.

Taking a deep breath, she changed the subject. "Daniel's on his way back home to Australia today."

"You must be terribly busy." Faith sent Daniel a saccharin smile. "We're sorry to have held you up. She's in good hands now."

Scarlet bristled. *In good hands now*...meaning she wasn't when she was with Daniel.

His handsome face was a mask. He'd caught Faith's slight but he had dignity enough not to lob one back. As his focus slid over to Scarlet and he sent her a quick wink, she projected a silent message.

As far as I'm concerned, I was in excellent hands.

He addressed her parents.

"Did you know your daughter wants to visit Australia?"

Faith shot her a look. "It's incredibly dusty."

"Getting dirty never hurt anyone," Scarlet returned.

Rubbing his chin, Daniel sauntered over to stand before the coffee table and its albums. "I wonder whether a few days away might help."

Eyeing Daniel, her father rearranged himself in his chair. "Help how?"

"Getting away," he explained. "Having some fun. Rather than trying to load her with information, it could be better to, you know, ease up."

Faith got to her feet. "We don't want to hold you up, Mr. McNeal. You must have a plane to catch."

"My jet's on standby."

Pushing out of her seat, her heart crashing beneath her ribs, Scarlet joined him. Had she heard him right? "Are you asking me to go with you to Australia?" She saw the smile in his eyes meant just for her.

"You said you wanted a holiday."

Cara shot to her feet, too. "I'll help you pack."

"It's out of the question," Faith said calmly.

Her father spoke up. "Daniel, we're grateful for your help up to this point, but, son, we don't know you."

"I can vouch for Daniel," Cara said. "He and Max have been friends forever. My fiancé would trust this man with his life."

Rolling her eyes, Faith muttered, "So dramatic."

Scarlet held on to a growl. She wanted to tell everyone to be quiet. She might be living in a void, but it was her life, her choice, and unless someone stepped in to declare her mentally incompetent she was going. But she was interested, too, to hear which way her father's opinion would fall.

Elbows on the chair arms, her father threaded his fingers at chest level and made an odd grunting sound, which flicked a faint light on in Scarlet's memory. He did that when he needed to voice a tough decision.

"It's well documented," her father said, "that good things can come from taking the pressure off."

Faith's jaw dropped. "You agree she should just run away?"

He stood. "I know you're concerned but I have a good feeling about this." Then he addressed Scarlet. "That is, if you want to go."

Scarlet's focus shot to Cara, who gave a quick nod. When her gaze met Daniel's, he grinned and shrugged. *Your choice.* Over near the unlit fireplace, Faith Anders had paled and looked set to collapse back into her chair. Scarlet didn't want to hurt anyone but the vote was four to one.

"I promise not to go swimming in any croc-infested lakes, Mom."

Faith blinked and a genuine smile breathed color back into her face. "You called me Mom."

Her father moved to link an arm around Faith's waist. He nodded and smiled encouragingly at his daughter before brushing a kiss over his wife's cheek.

That's when Scarlet had a flash of insight. She might not remember these people but, in this house, she knew that she was loved.

From the sidelines, Daniel watched Scarlet take stock of the interior of her town house. Her expression was curious but it didn't look as if any lights were blinking on. One moment she was concentrating on the piano, then a framed shot of her folks displayed in the middle of the mantel. Next minute she pivoted away and almost stumbled on the potted palm, which she clearly hadn't remembered being there. She knocked over a poker by the fireplace and had to steady herself, her two hands braced against the wall. For the first time since her topple yesterday, real frustration tightened her mouth.

Flustered, Scarlet set her tote bag down heavily on a nearby timber sideboard. The bag tipped over, upending a delicate porcelain figurine of a teenage girl embracing an armful of flowers. Swooping, Scarlet caught the figurine before it hit the floor. Her face ashen now, she moved to set the piece carefully back in place. Daniel noticed her hands were shaking.

As he joined her, she pasted on a weak smile and wound a sweep of hair behind one ear.

"That looks expensive," she said. "Probably would've hated myself later if it'd smashed."

Settling a calming palm on her back, he examined the living room. Decorated very much like the senior Anderses' home, it featured lots of paneled wood, tasteful embroidered furnishings, expensive traditional touches like fine artwork and display crystal. *Whatever floats your boat.*

"Anything look familiar?" he asked.

"Nothing." She traced fingertips along the polished sideboard's rim. "But I'm not entirely uncomfortable."

That was good. Promising. "Maybe you should rethink Down Under and stay here with Cara instead."

"What you said at my parents' made sense. I'd like to get away. Let my brain breathe instead of have it loaded down. But it was a rather random announcement, Daniel. I thought I'd been crowding you."

Not crowding. She'd been giving his conscience a good poke. Putting him between a rock and one very hard place. When they'd first met, he'd wanted to see more of her. What they'd shared last night had, frankly, blown him away. Placing her outside of temptation's way seemed like a plan. However…

"Your parents obviously mean well but, from where I stood, they were only confusing you more." His palm fanned between her shoulder blades. "And there was an element of self-interest attached to my suggestion."

She turned to face him. Her eyes glittered into his as she gave him a sly smile. "Are you suggesting we pick up where we left off? Because I'm certain there's a bedroom around here somewhere."

When she leaned toward him, his neurons started firing signals, preparing him for contact. But now was not the time for play. He caught her arms.

"My pilot's issued a departure time. We should try to keep it."

Her eyes narrowed as she considered the logistics. "I wonder what vacation clothes I have," she said softly to herself as she sauntered away.

When she disappeared up the staircase, he followed her. Should he mention that when she wasn't concentrating so hard, she seemed to know her way around?

Upstairs consisted of two pristine bedrooms and their attached baths. Daniel watched Scarlet enter the main suite, cross straight to the walk-in closet and throw open the doors. When he caught up, she stood examining neat rows of clothes and shoes. Everything was color coded. Skirts and trousers were to one side, blouses to the other. Dresses hung, evenly spaced, in the middle.

She let out a long impressed whistle. "I sure do have good taste. And these shoes are amazing. I must spend all my money at boutiques."

"Any bikinis?" he asked eagerly then cleared his throat. "We'll be spending a lot of time on the water."

After digging around in drawers, pulling stuff out, leaving other bits and pieces hanging, she gave up. "Nothing," she said. Then she considered the exposed lengths of her arms as if she'd never seen them before. "I am fair. Maybe I don't have a swimsuit because I don't go in the sun."

"New invention. It's called sunblock."

She nodded at the pants section. "I have a pair of jeans but nothing else that says casual. No flip-flops, not even with platforms and sparkles." She threw up her hands. "What kind of person has no regular weekend clothes?"

"Gee, I don't know." His shoulder butted against the jamb. "A person who looks amazing in Versace?"

She cast him an appreciative smile. "Thanks, but I'd feel more at home in cutoffs."

"I'm happy when you're wearing nothing." He blinked. "And I didn't just say that."

"Because I really hated hearing it." Her teeth tugging at her lower lip, she closed the distance separating them. "Are you sure we can't spare a few minutes to check out that bed?"

"Do you really believe either one of us would want to stop at a few minutes?" He spied a piece of luggage on the shelf above their heads. He swung the case down and nudged it toward her. "Throw together a few things. I'll take you shopping when we get home."

She tapped his chest. "You're on."

She opened a different set of drawers. Daniel groaned. Sexy lingerie city. Maybe the old Scarlet wasn't hopelessly repressed, after all.

She angled around, swirling an X-rated thong on an index finger.

"Narrow, black and lacy." Dangling the G-string at an appropriate level, she rocked her hips. "I appreciate the loan of Morgan's underwear but these look like a lot more fun."

He realized he was nodding, leaning forward, growing harder. With a start, he shot the case up under his chin. "You won't get me to change my mind."

"No?"

Shoulders hunching, he lifted the case higher still.

"No."

"Then turn your head. I need to change."

She proceeded to peel her T-shirt up over her head. Daniel swallowed. She wasn't wearing a bra. He set down the case heavily.

"That's it. I'm calling the tease police."

But she was busy dragging off her trousers and briefs. Sweat broke out along the dent of his spine. "It's way too hot in here."

She crossed to him and, without any further provocation, his mouth dropped over hers. The tip of her tongue played with his as she unbuttoned his shirt, then filed her fingers up through the hair on his chest. When she let him come up for air, he gripped her hips and issued a warning.

"If you're going to take advantage of me again, it'll need to be quick."

She dotted sweet kisses on his chest, then slid lower onto her knees. The metal sound of his zipper easing down had him gripping the doorjambs to either side of him. She lowered his briefs, and cool air hit before the moist warmth of her mouth circled, then drew him in. Daniel's hold on the jambs tightened.

This was going to be one hell of a trip.

Eight

Scarlet took a sip of her ice water, stole a glance at the person sitting opposite. Finally she cleared her throat.

"I haven't thanked you yet."

Morgan Tibbs dragged her attention from her *Forbes* magazine. "This is Daniel's jet," she said. "Not mine."

"I mean for the clothes." The briefs.

"Oh. Thought they might come in handy."

Morgan went back to her magazine and Scarlet went back to sipping water.

"Suppose I should feel weird," Scarlet finally said, "flying halfway around the world with people I barely know in a luxury private jet, but it's no weirder than what I've lived through these past twenty-four hours."

"The amnesia?"

"Uh-huh."

Morgan put down her *Forbes*. "I have an aunt who experienced a fugue state. She worked as a headmistress. When she didn't show up for duty for a couple of days, a search team went out looking for her. She was found over a hundred miles away, meditating with a peace-loving group who were waiting for aliens to land in the parking lot. My aunt had no clue about her previous life. Seems her husband, who'd faked his own death twenty years earlier, had shown up on her doorstep. The shock set her off."

"Did her memory come back?"

"Pretty much as soon as they got her home."

"That didn't happen for me."

"No sparks at all?"

"A few things. Sure."

Morgan ran a finger and thumb over the six studs in her right ear. "Maybe this is your mind's way of telling you to take a break."

"I seem to have nice enough parents who obviously care about me. I have a nice home. A good job. From all accounts, great friends."

"Sounds neat. A great life to go back to." She lifted her magazine. "And yet here you are, flying away from it all."

Daniel came strolling down the aisle.

"Morgan, these figures don't add up. Can you go over the analysis of per capita spread based on age and socioeconomic demographic and let me know if your median is anywhere near mine?"

"Love to."

Morgan slinked out of her seat, took his laptop and disappeared.

When Scarlet was sure Morgan was out of earshot, she whispered, "Is she being facetious?"

"Always." Daniel took the seat next to her. "And she's the best right-hand man/person/woman I've ever had."

Scarlet's smile faded.

"Daniel, do you think that this amnesia thing could be self-inflicted?"

"What? Like you meant to trip and knock yourself out?"

"Like some part of my brain is purposely forgetting?"

"As vast as our universe is, our brains are just as immeasurable."

Scarlet drank that in. So he was saying maybe she had, maybe she hadn't. She didn't feel as if she was putting on an act. She knew what she knew and the most important thing was that she felt safe with him. She wouldn't be here if she didn't. Even if her mother had seemed annoyed that their daughter should upset society by doing what she felt was right.

"I didn't know you very well," she said, "did I? And yet my gut tells me you know me better than everyone else combined. Why is that?"

His smile was soothing. Sexy.

"I'm not a doctor."

"You're my friend," she countered. "Aren't you?"

"Sure I'm your friend."

But his smile said he wasn't convinced.

"In other words," she decided, "I should just sit back, enjoy the champagne and all-expenses-paid vacation and quit worrying."

"That would be my best advice. But then you're more pedantic than that."

She searched her brain for clues. "Pedantic as in O.C.D.-ish?"

"You have goals."

"Well, that's good," she announced, but he only looked away. "Unless they're bad goals?"

"Or someone else's."

"My parents'?"

He turned to face her. "Scarlet, you were recently engaged. A few days ago you called off the relationship."

"You're kidding. I was getting married?"

"You decided he wasn't right for you."

"Wow. Hope I didn't break his heart too much."

Daniel's gaze shuttered.

"Does he know about my fall?" she asked, all the more curious. "About my memory loss?"

"Before we left your parents' house, your dad pulled me aside. He'd contacted Everett Matheson to pass on the news."

She tried to remember but the name didn't ring any bells. "And?"

"And your ex said he was busy in New York."

Emotion hit her chest, took her breath. In the recesses of her brain, she remembered a man's pompous sounding laughter. It made her shudder.

"He wasn't concerned?" she asked. "Not at all?"

Daniel reached across, held her hand. "Don't worry. He didn't deserve you."

They flew directly into Sydney, dropped Morgan off, then went on to Cairns. They cruised an hour and a half in a convertible down the Bruce Highway to Port Hinchinbrook heaven. When she walked into the open-plan lower story of his extravagant beach house and was greeted by that amazing panoramic view of the ocean, she gasped.

"This is like paradise. Why would anyone ever want to live anywhere else?"

"You haven't been out on the yacht yet."

"You are so incredibly lucky."

He thought about that. He wished his childhood had been different. Normal. But he didn't live in the past. He'd moved on. Made his own luck.

She was studying her arms. "I put sunblock on for that brilliant drive with the top down but I need more. I'm dying to go walk along the shoreline." She spun to face him. "I need a swimsuit."

"Let's see what we can do."

He ushered her up the stairs.

The top story was a huge open-plan bedroom. Laid out on the bed, draped over partitions and furniture, was the wardrobe he and Morgan had secretly put together online during the flight over.

She covered her open mouth with her hands. "This is all for me?" She headed for the nearest lot of dresses, studied some price tags and held on to a nearby chair for support. "This is crazy. Obscene! You must have spent a fortune."

"You are a woman who likes quality clothing, remember?"

"Not really." Her face broke into that unabashed smile he loved. "But I won't argue."

As he watched her dance around the room, twirling with various garments held against her and swinging by to press a big kiss on his cheek, a feeling ribboned through him, bright and uncommonly close. He'd bought people gifts before—he enjoyed being generous—but he couldn't remember anyone being so unrestrained in showing their appreciation. She was like a kid on Christmas morning. This everyday girl was happy, and she had no qualms about letting the world know it. He loved her exuberance. Her open, almost reckless brand of affection.

Honestly, he'd be sad when this Scarlet disappeared.

"If you don't like anything, we'll return it," he said, concentrating on enjoying the here and now.

"Don't you dare! I adore every single piece." Her exuberant expression become more contemplative as she studied him. "You're always this thoughtful, aren't you? You like surprising people. Seeing them happy."

Wringing villainous hands, he advanced. "Ah, but I can be ruthlessly selfish, too."

"You should probably show me that side to compare."

Lord knows, he was thinking the same.

She blindly set aside the colorful frock she held and they came together in the middle of the room, the sunshine radiating in through the northern wall of glass warming the contact all the more. Her arms circled his back, while he gathered her up in his, and a split second later their mouths joined. At last he was kissing her again.

Since that bone-melting scene in her walk-in closet, he'd doubled his efforts to keep his distance from Scarlet in that physical sense. He'd had visions of being cornered on the plane and, as cool as Morgan was, he didn't need to put her in an awkward position. Nothing would have been more embarrassing than his assistant being forced to watch the enraptured couple make out.

Restraint had been called for. All that wanting to feel Scarlet's skin pressed up against his had to wait. He'd contented himself with the occasional hand on her shoulder, a casual brushing of arms as they passed. Even when they'd slipped into his convertible in the airport long-term parking lot and were alone again, he'd kept his hands on the wheel.

Now, Daniel unleashed his pent-up need. He couldn't wait to get their clothes off. He wanted to have her naked, writhing beneath him. Then he wanted a replay with positions reversed. And that was just the beginning.

His mouth covering hers, he began to unbutton her blouse. But the holes were tight and the buttons numerous and small. Frustrating.

Really very annoying.

He broke the kiss to actually see what he was doing. Even then, it was agonizingly slow going. Why wasn't Scarlet taking charge or at least helping? She only stood there patiently while he grew increasingly aggravated at the tiny pearl beads. His fingers had never been this clumsy before.

"You want me to suffer," he surmised.

"How does it feel?"

She was getting him back?

"Morgan puts up with a lot," he said. "It was best we showed some self-control in the air."

She checked out his progress, his ever more urgent tugs at her blouse. "How's that self-control working for you now?"

He ripped the blouse open. Pearl buttons popped, spitting shrapnel at his chest, onto the floor.

"Obviously not well," he said, spreading the fabric, exposing her breasts. He paused. "You're not wearing a bra."

She was winding her arms out of her blouse. "Apparently I don't like them."

Those words came to him muffled, as if she'd spoken through a pillow. All his energies were concentrated on admiring her body, sculpting the shape of her perfect breasts with his hands, telling himself he ought to cut to the chase and rip off her jeans, too.

"How desperate were you to visit the beach?" he asked in between grazing his lips up the slope of her neck.

"After sitting for so long I thought we could use the exercise," she murmured, running her fingers through his hair.

"Exercise comes in many and varied forms. Did you know that simply taking one's clothes off can burn eight to ten calories?" He nipped her earlobe. "Vigorous sexual intercourse burns four hundred." He stole another kiss…a thorough, make-no-mistake tongue-on-tongue assault. "Of course," he said, coming up for air, "the best way to ensure you get a great work out is to—"

"Orgasm?"

He grinned against her lips. "As many times as possible."

Capturing her mouth again with his, he herded her toward the bed while he ran his palms down her bare back and threaded his fingers into her jeans. When the backs of her legs hit the foot of the bed, she broke the kiss and dragged in a lungful of air.

"Have you worked up a sweat yet?"

He was unbuttoning her jeans. "I'm more interested in your metabolic rate."

His fingers snaked down into that warm, soft, wet place. Her head lolled to the side and her hips tipped forward. While his other palm feathered up to cup her jaw, he scooped two fingers deep inside, between her folds.

She hummed out a smile. As he dropped kisses over the shell of her ear, across her brow, her pelvis tilted toward him more and more until she was grinding. His own fires were building, too. His erection was pounding, aching to take over.

As she moved with him, he remembered his view from on high of her kneeling before him, taking him fully into her mouth. He recalled the pressure when she'd held and gently squeezed him. He'd never forget warning her it was almost too late and how she'd worked even harder before he had time to withdraw. During the flight, he'd kept his hands to himself but he'd given a lot of thought to giving her the same kind of pleasure. She'd approved of the clothes. He hoped that she'd like what he had in mind for her now even more.

She was clinging to his shirt when her climax broke. As spasms rocked through her, one delicate hand dropped and clamped over his. Her head rocked back and, eyes shut tight, she snatched back air and gave herself over to each wave of throbbing heat.

He didn't allow her time to float down, recover. Instead, he eased her back onto his bed. With her bottom near the edge and legs loosely dangling over the side, he wrangled off her jeans and scrap of silk underwear. Hunkering down, he urged her knees wide apart and positioned himself between them. The sight of her glistening and swollen was enough to send him into spasms. With a palm set on each inner thigh, he used his thumbs to open her more and expose her nub. Then he lowered his head and, relishing each stroke, brought her to climax again.

The next day was gorgeous. "A real beauty," Daniel called it. Flawless skies. Little wind. Perfect glassy seas.

From the back entrance of his amazing Hinchinbrook holiday home, Daniel showed her down the southern drive across the road and some parkland—which he apparently owned but had donated to the community—to a hundred-foot pontoon. The yacht was a jaw-dropper.

"Presidents have yachts less impressive than this," she pointed out.

"A friend of mine owns the company," he said, as if that explained it. He opened the back deck door and, with a flourish, gestured her aboard. "Let's go sailing."

Floppy hat on, sunblock well applied, she followed as he climbed a set of fiberglass stairs to the fly bridge. Beneath a canopy, amid a gentle balmy breeze, she stood back and watched as he turned a key, pushed the throttles and steered them out into the passage.

"We'll cruise at around ten knots," he said, while she studied his classic profile and the cute way his hair licked off his collar. "We'll pass Hinchinbrook Island in thirty minutes."

As they slid out over a vast expanse of sun-kissed water, Scarlet held on to the rail and, breathing in the heady scent of fresh salty air, tried to cement herself in this tropical paradise reality. This was another world. Another time. Who needed D.C., its politics and all its watch-your-back traffic? She only wanted to get around barefoot. Wanted to hang on to this sublime sense of freedom.

"Tell me about this place," she said. "It reminds me of Tahiti."

He gave her a sharp look. "Is that from a personal memory?"

Or from books, internet ads, photos from traveling friends? She came up a blank. "I'm not sure."

Frowning, he concentrated on the ocean again.

"The island up ahead is approximately thirty-eight kilometers long and ten meters wide."

Twenty-four miles by around six, she thought.

"It has eleven beaches that all belong on postcards or travel agency walls. The national park covers thirty-nine thousand hectares. A hundred acres of natural heaven."

"You know your facts."

Strong bronzed arms extended, hands on the wheel, he flashed over a grin. "I've played tour host before."

For visitors to his Port Hinchinbrook home. Guests on this yacht. Female guests? Of course Daniel had a life before now. He was hardly a priest. Clearly he enjoyed female company. To be fair, she must have had previous lovers, too. Everett the ex for one. But whenever she studied him, looking so commanding and sailor-sexy at the helm, she shunned imagining him with anyone else. Or speculating about whom he might hook up with once this unusual affair was done.

And it *would* end. Her memory would return and their differences would come to light again. Differences that scratched at the back of her mind every now and then. He came from one world—this open carefree realm. And she came from another—one that was reflected in her parents' regal home, the immaculate clothes hanging in her wardrobe.

Reaching open water, the engines revved higher and the ancient island drew nearer. The hills and heavy verdant foliage looked untouched.

"Are visitors allowed?" she asked.

"Hinchinbrook Island has a resort, but only a limited amount of visitors are allowed on the trails each year." Muscles jumped in his arms as he veered the boat marginally to the left. "We'll visit another day," he said. "You need to see the reef."

They sailed farther out while she absorbed the surrounding beauty of sea and sky as well as the captain. The telling kink on one side of Daniel's mouth said this was a big part of what he loved most. This was one of the pleasures he lived for. And as her body rocked with the slap of twin bows against water and she breathed in nature at its quintessential best, she imagined herself enjoying this life day after day. Being with Daniel like this all the time. Then she remembered what she knew of her life in D.C. and she simply couldn't see the two ever melding.

Soon Daniel was easing back on the throttles. The surrounding water was crystalline. Transparent. Farther out, shelves of coral came into view. With its many vibrant colors, this living, breathing wonderland seemed to lie just below the surface. She saw multiple schools of fish darting around their playground. She couldn't wait to dive in and swim around, too.

A whirring, clanking sound vibrated beneath them. The anchor, she guessed, lowered to the floor of the sea—not onto the coral—to keep them in place. Daniel shut off the engine and rubbed his hands.

"Let's get wet."

Ten minutes later they were geared up and splashing off the side of the yacht into water that was the ideal temperature. She wore an exquisite watermelon-colored one-piece, one of the many items of clothing generously supplied by her host. Daniel wore swim shorts that made her think of James Bond and that incredible beach scene. Although she'd take her gorgeous geek over 007 any day.

While they swished their flippers, keeping vertically afloat, Daniel showed her how to clear her mask and use the snorkel hose. When she swam down to the coral, she should let her hose fill with water, he said. Returning to the surface, she needed to "blast clear" the water from the tube with a sharp exhalation.

"That plateau," she said, peering down while she waved her legs and flippers, "it looks close enough to touch from here."

"You can swim on the surface," he said, "or hold your breath, dive down and really get in there."

A huge groper glided past below her feet and an alarm sounded in her head. "Should I be scared?"

He laughed. "You should be excited."

The next hour was spent drifting near the coral. So many brilliant hues and fascinating shapes…fans and fingers and flowers…cones, pancakes and igniting stars. Fish featuring as many colors and forms swirled around, sometimes straight up to her mask to have a closer look, other times grazing her legs, even nibbling her fingers when she held them out.

On another plane, she knew she didn't normally like the sun and outdoor sport, but this was different. Here with Daniel she felt at home. Whenever she surfaced and cleared her hose, she only wanted to dive straight back down and weave among the inhabitants of this tranquil submarine world.

Underwater, through his mask, Daniel caught her eye and gestured upward. Feeling light and surreal, she shot to the surface. He slid back his mask.

"We should eat. Have a rest."

"I'm not tired."

"You're hooked?"

"I can't wait to do it again."

"For now, let's get you out of the sun for a while."

Daniel had had the fridge stocked ahead of time. They enjoyed cheese and pâté, then the finest selection of seafood Scarlet had ever tasted. The shrimp were salty and überfresh. Oysters were huge and too delicious to talk about. Sweetest melon—pink and orange—melted on her tongue. Leaning back in the shade of the deck, she wondered if there could possibly be a better life. A more handsome companion. A stronger wish to keep things between them just as they were now.

He was pouring more water; apparently keeping fluids up was superimportant. His hair had dried in a series of dark-blond spikes and his broad bare shoulders were laced with traces of sea salt. As he handed over a plastic cup, she longed to tell him how perfectly happy she was. It was an exuberant, although slightly melancholy, feeling.

She might never be this happy again.

An all-encompassing shadow passed over the deck. Overhead a series of clouds were drifting in. Gauging the sky, she took two mouthfuls of water.

"Do you get many bad storms?" she asked.

"A couple of years ago," he said, setting down his cup, "a cyclone swept through here. Ripped the town up. Houses were torn down. Boats lay piled up on top of one another on the harbor like crumpled cards. We had some time to prepare before it hit. A few of us holed up in a shelter I had built a little inland."

"You deliberately stayed? Weren't you terrified?"

Far as she knew, cyclones, hurricanes, typhoons—they were pretty much the same. Essentially violent storms sweeping in from the ocean. If she'd owned a private jet, she'd have gotten her family and friends together and flown as far away as possible.

"It was scary," he said. "The constant crashing. We stayed in the shelter until the winds eased. The scene outside was devastating. The footage I took was the first of its kind and was re-Waved around the world. When I got home, there was a thirty-foot boat anchored in the second-story window."

Trying to imagine that kind of force, she glanced around.

"It's hard to believe this calm could turn into something so vicious. It's so quiet now."

"It sometimes happens like that," he said, leaning over and dropping a kiss on her cheek. "There's the quiet. Then there's the storm."

Like the one she felt slowly building inside of her. Memories—small, fragmented—were creeping back in. How soon before they all came together? She only hoped that when they did, all hell didn't break loose.

Late in the afternoon, a bale of turtles befriended them.

Scarlet sat on the back bench, her chin resting on the ledge of her folded arms as she leaned on the deck's fiberglass rail and gazed, entranced, over the edge. Aside from being on the open road on his motorbike, this was the place Daniel felt most at peace. Out here he didn't need to think about business or the world's mounting problems. When he powered out to sea, he forgot about everything but the lap of water against the hull and the blessed heat of the Capricorn sun on his skin.

During this trip he'd enjoyed the company of a woman who had seemed as enthralled by the experience as he was. And every time he looked at her, his evaluation of Scarlet Anders changed a little more and he saw something different. Something innocent, unique and begging to be set free, and not for just a day but for the rest of her time on this earth. Everyone deserved the chance to feel this natural. To be themselves.

An increasing stirring breeze caught her hair and swirled it around her head like a living river of gold. Catching it, she spied him studying her. Her smile was wide, white and trusting. Frankly, the message it sent melted his heart. Angling around to face him, she rearranged the silk beach shirttails around her thighs.

His fingertips tingled. Other than pecks, he hadn't kissed

her the entire time they'd been out here. Perhaps he ought to remedy that.

"Mr. Daniel McNeal," she announced. "Your ancestry's obviously Irish."

About to head over and join her, his head kicked back. He didn't want to spoil the day by bringing up subjects like his history. But hers was a guileless query. She was curious, even if he'd sooner forget his last name was McNeal.

On his feet, he dug a cloth out from a nearby compartment and began polishing a stainless-steel fitting. "My father's ancestry was Irish."

"I love the accent. So friendly. Kind of lilting. Did your mother fall in love with him at first sight?"

"I believe it was mutual."

Arching a brow, she leaned elbows back over the rail. "And?"

"And they married quickly," he said, moving to the next fitting to shine that up bright. "Had a son."

"And named him Daniel." Her head cocked. "My dad looks so…nondescript. So by the book. I bet your father was a character."

A character? That was one way of putting it.

"He liked to work hard." He'd already told her that, although she wouldn't remember. Vigorously rubbing the stainless steel, he sent over a quick grin. "He wanted to save for a rainy day."

"Did a rainy day ever come?"

His cloth stopped moving. He wanted to brush the subject off. But he'd already decided. When they hit Sydney, he would take Scarlet along when he visited his foster dad—the man who had been like a father to him for twenty-odd years. So he'd have to explain at least some of his past.

"When I was five, my father lost his job. Not because of performance," he pointed out; he wanted to be fair. "It was a corporate cost-cutting measure, the type that's really caught on these days. You know, where companies chase higher profit margins to keep stockholders happy, which equates to workers, many with families, being flicked like the stub of a used cigarette. As for my father, small jobs dribbled in," he went on, "but not enough to pay the bills. My father..." His gut swooped and kicked. This was harder then he'd thought. "Well...he changed."

She crossed the deck and laid a supportive hand on his arm. "Everyone deserves the right to work, to earn a decent living."

Absolutely. He might own a billion-dollar company but he made damn sure his staff was treated well and received the highest benefits. Every employee from Morgan Tibbs to a night-duty cleaner was given respect and rewarded for a job well done.

"My father grew sullen," Daniel said, absently running his cloth back and forth over the stainless steel as he thought back. "He started to drink. He'd always enjoyed a shandy. Half beer, half lemonade. But he was home a lot now, spending all his time in the shed or down the pub. I think whiskey made him forget. It also made him violent."

Scarlet squeezed his arm. He wanted to smile and say it was okay. His father never really hurt anyone. Only that wasn't true.

That same prickly, sick feeling swelled in his chest, clogging his throat. It came whenever he thought too long about "back then." He wanted to push the nausea, the anger, away but he wasn't finished telling Scarlet what she needed to know. Not everything, of course. The abridged version was crappy enough.

"My father did things he couldn't recall doing in the morning," Daniel said as a darker cloud covered the sun and the temperature on deck cooled a degree. "One day my mother told him to leave." He remembered her screaming at him to get out, get out, *get out!* He used to dream about it. Night-mares that had left him shaking. "The old man moved out. But every other night he'd sneak in my window, sit on the edge my bed and promise me this wasn't forever. I'd smell hard liquor on his breath. Days of sweat on his clothes. I wanted him to come home, but I didn't want him home like that."

He hadn't meant to go into that much detail. But by say-ing it aloud, he realized he should have told his mother about those midnight visits. It had never occurred to him to tattle-tale; he'd kept all those dark feelings to himself.

"I wish I could go back to that time and give you a great big hug." Scarlet pressed closer. "And they both died when you were young?"

"I was fostered out to a man by the name of Owen Cedar."

"A good man?"

"Very good. I'll take you to meet him when we're in Syd-ney."

"And your biological dad—"

"I don't think about it," he said, tossing the polishing rag aside. "That's all in the past."

He wiped at the sweat that had broken out on the back of his neck. Damn, he wished the temperature would drop a few more degrees.

An answer from above! Dots of rain began hitting the deck and, beyond that, made tiny expanding circles in the water. He peered into the depths. The turtles were gone.

"We need to get going."

Her face filled with disappointment. "Couldn't we just go inside?"

And ride out the squall? He reached for her, brushed his mouth over hers, felt her quiver in response. And a good mea-sure of those bad feelings—the remnants of those unpleas-ant memories—disappeared. He threaded an arm around her waist and guided her through into the cabin.

They needed a shower to wash the salt off. He intended to clean every grain from her body, then personally pat every inch dry.

As the wind whipped around them and she held on to Daniel's leather-clad back, Scarlet couldn't believe that she'd been such a baby about getting on and riding this beast.

They'd already spent three days cruising the Great Ocean Road on Daniel's motorbike and she wasn't certain which she'd enjoyed more—this amazing road adventure or those tranquil days spent up north on the ocean.

They'd stayed on at Port Hinchinbrook three days. A great deal of the time was spent on the yacht, visiting the reef and their regular turtle fans. Daniel had shown her Hinchinbrook Island, too. Together they'd strolled along breathtakingly beautiful beaches, spotting dolphins jumping in the bay and taking in a glorious sunset from the lookout.

On the fourth day, they'd flown down to Victoria, Australia's most southern east-coast state. His prized bike was waiting for them there, garaged at one end of the Great Ocean Road, a span of highway that wound along Victoria's lower rim. Daniel had been champing at the bit to get going. But she'd hesitated. There were no seat belts. No car cabin to provide protection.

Now Scarlet hung on tighter and, pressing her front closer to Daniel's back, reveled in the sense of liberty that two fast wheels and a sexy billionaire could provide. As they swerved around a bend and another picturesque bay came into view over the rise, she rested her cheek against his shoulder blade and thanked the powers that be for the fall that had led to this adventure.

But the memories were coming back.

Snippets about her life in D.C., parts about her parents and starting up the business with Ariella. Her brain hadn't yet released information about that first meeting with Daniel. Some foggy recollection of being unhappy with him at a recent black-tie function was filtering back…she was telling him they shouldn't be together because…

Because…well, she didn't know all of it yet.

And she hadn't let on that her memory was coming back. She didn't want Daniel wondering when all the swirling pieces would eventually fall into place. She'd sooner enjoy their time together without that complication. Right now she only wanted freedom. Wanted fun. This other world.

They'd visited places with soaring rock stacks, majestic monster cliffs, crashing surf as well as peaceful bays and lush forests. On a bushwalk, they'd come across koala after koala sleeping, perched in the forks of gum trees. She'd never forget the fresh smell of eucalypt, the supersoft fabric of the koalas' fur beneath her fingertips.

They'd also watched people taking surf lessons, another of Daniel's hobbies. He took short videos featuring some of the amazing sights, of her petting a wallaby and ducking as a flock of king parrots swooped and squawked. He posted photos along with captions on Waves. As if he didn't have enough followers already, his numbers went through the roof. Everyone wanted to comment. Everyone wanted to see where they'd be next. They wanted to know the name of the lady he was with, the woman whose face he was careful to conceal.

They stopped at inexpensive hotels or bed-and-breakfasts along the way. On this, their third day, he pulled the bike off the road near a quiet horseshoe beach and hand in hand they walked down to the sand. Waves rolled in. The huge orange ball of sun was sinking behind them. As she gazed out over the water, inhaling the salty air and feeling the cool breeze on her cheeks, he stood behind her and wrapped his arms around her.

"Beautiful, isn't it?" He murmured against her ear. "Almost as beautiful as you."

Her eyes watered because of the wind, but more so because of a surge of emotion. She held on to his arms, hugging them and pressing her back against his solid frame.

"I should tell Max to bring Cara here for their honeymoon," he said. "I could make it my wedding gift to them. That could be my surprise." He chuckled. "I'm definitely mellowing."

And for some reason that was all it took for those missing pieces to spring to vivid life in her mind and fall into place. She remembered him showing up at DC Affairs when she was hanging the cupids. She remembered the roses and bow-tied kangaroo. More than anything she remembered their first steamy kiss. And—

Oh, God. She remembered it all.

Nine

Standing speechless on the back balcony of Daniel's Sydney home, Scarlet swept her gaze over a panoramic view that could only be described as humbling.

"This must be the most beautiful city in the world," she said as Daniel moved from the open French doors to join her.

The giant shells of the Opera House, surrounded on three sides by water, made a statement about architectural genius and parochial pride. The cityscape on their left looked young and bold and full of life. Sydney Harbour itself was so vast and picture-book blue.

"You should stand here on New Year's Eve," he said. "So many boats and crowds lining the shoreline." He pointed out the Harbour Bridge in the distance. "At midnight the bridge fireworks go off and the entire sky is filled with endless explosions of light and color."

She pointed to a spire, a structure that reminded her of the Washington Monument back home.

"It's called the Sydney Tower Eye," Daniel explained. "The turret holds close to a thousand people."

"It looks amazingly high."

"It's also ranked as one of the safest buildings in the world. Each year hundreds participate in the Tower Run-up, a charity event that involves racing up 1,504 steps to the top. It raises money for beach safety."

"Which brings me to something I *must* see. Where's Bondi Beach?"

He hooked a thumb over his shoulder. "Across the other way. We'll go have an ice cream and sit on the sand tomorrow."

She studied his home's manicured lawns sprawling out toward harborside parkland. Wide stone steps led from the lower story of the house to a massive triangular pool. He'd given a tour of the building—it was big and luxurious. But the style didn't fit with her understanding of his tastes. Turning around, she studied what she could of the rear of the house.

"When was this place built?"

"An entrepreneur had it made to order in the twenties. He wasn't five feet tall but he became a giant in business... farming, newspapers. It's had a few owners in between, but the first time I drove through the gates, walked in the front door, I felt the energy. The view was a bonus."

"You should have someone commission a painting."

"Know anyone good?"

She almost provided a name but bit her lip.

Her memory was back—*everything*. But she needed to find the right time to tell him. When she'd taken up his offer to fly away—to escape—she'd accepted a part of herself that she never would have dreamed existed. Impulsive. Impassioned. Because of this experience—because of what Daniel had given her these past days—she was a different person. More balanced. Less black and white.

Of course, she couldn't hide away here with him forever. Soon this amazing holiday would need to come to an end. But how would she broach the subject and confess that every one of her memories had returned and she hadn't said a word?

Daniel had slanted an arm behind her on the rail. Now he tilted toward her, tracing his lips over her crown, dropping slow purposeful kisses on her temple. Closing her eyes, Scarlet let herself relax as his other arm wound around her front, his palm grazing the exposed band of skin above her jeans. When his fingers trailed lower, she quivered and didn't think about tomorrow.

"Want to go for a ride around the harbor?" he asked.

Scarlet heard more the sexy growl in his voice than the question. She roused herself enough to respond.

"Hmm. What did you say?"

"Ferries crisscross all over the place. We could spend the afternoon on the north shore at Luna Park." His fingertips skimmed her belly, then dipped lower still. "Or we could stay in."

In her haze, she slowly smiled. Staying in sounded divine. But a name he'd mentioned had stuck in her mind. She'd heard about Australia's most famous amusement park, its huge smiley face entrance, and she remembered…

She turned around. "Wasn't there an accident there years ago?" Before he could ask, she explained, "I'm not sure…I might have read about it somewhere once."

He was looking at her curiously, clearly wondering what else she might have recalled. "There was an accident. In the Ghost Train tunnel."

"People were killed."

"That was forty years ago. Everything's updated. Regularly safety checked."

She listened as he explained how the rides had been removed, restored and, in some cases, redesigned. How nothing like that had ever happened since. Still...

She held his sandpapery jaw in two hands. "Is it okay if we don't do any roller coasters today?"

He chuckled. "Where's my little thrill seeker?" he asked.

She's being moderated by the more sensible mature me, Scarlet thought. But she wouldn't tell him that. Not yet. She'd choose the best time for this spell to be broken, even if she felt guilty about keeping the truth from him in the meantime.

She changed the subject.

"Weren't we going to see your dad?" Daniel had mentioned he wanted to catch up. Then she remembered to qualify her words. "I mean, your foster dad."

Daniel did want to drop by and see Owen. He'd give him a call soon. But first he needed to satisfy a craving, one that seemed to grow more powerful every day. With Scarlet looking as if she had something to share, he lowered his head and imparted a kiss that only left him aching for more. Deep, thorough, but also steeped in meaning.

He was glad she didn't want to do the sightseeing thing today. Not that he wouldn't enjoy showing her the unique sights and sounds of his city—seeing her eyes widen in wonder and hearing her tinkling laughter each time he introduced her to something new. But tasting her again now, feeling her so supple and giving against him, he wanted to take her to bed first. He intended to relieve her of her clothes, cloak her body in caresses, before considering anything else.

Except making that call.

Reluctantly he broke the kiss and left Scarlet to pore over the view. Pulling out his cell, he moved inside and down a hall that led to the master suite. While he waited for Owen to answer the phone, Daniel considered the way Scarlet had returned his kiss just now. Her more uninhibited moods got his blood pumping so hard, restraint was an enormous challenge. But these past twenty-four hours or so, he'd been just as okay with her inclination toward "less explosive, more thoughtful."

Even cautious.

Which linked to her hesitation over doing Luna Park when a few days ago she'd have been first in line to volunteer for a base jump. And she'd recalled reading about an accident from almost half a century ago? So she'd regained some memories. Some understanding of who she'd been before. If that were the case, it made sense that she'd be feeling unsettled or cautious now, caught and even torn between two realities—pre- and postamnesia Scarlet. She might be wondering how she'd let Daniel talk her into flying away so far from home.

Before her fall, she didn't want to see him again. She'd called him a sports-mad, unconventional playboy who was only interested in pursuing pleasure. Her complete opposite. With recollections filtering back, was she secretly shocked at how close they'd become? How very intimate they'd been?

Wandering into the bedroom, he pulled back the bed covers and was in the master bath flicking on the indoor hot tub's faucet when his call connected. His foster dad laughed when he heard Daniel's voice.

"I'm in town," Daniel said.

"What are you doing tonight?"

"Visiting you."

"Perfect. I'm hosting a bush dance."

"Raising money for one of your community causes?"

"Whenever I can."

Although Owen refused any kind of handout himself, in the past he had suggested charities Daniel might want to assist with a spare buck or two. That's how he'd come across Youth Rules, among others.

"So it'll be all country music?" The squeak of a fiddle made him cringe. "No chance of slipping in a bit of rock?"

"What if we take a vote?"

And Daniel knew if he brought it up again, Owen would do just that. Owen always listened. He was always fair.

"Mind if I bring a friend?" Daniel asked.

"As long as she can promenade and do-si-do!"

Daniel didn't ask why his dad thought his friend was a woman. Over the years, Owen knew his foster son had enjoyed the company of more than a few ladies. But Daniel had never felt the kind of connection he'd formed with Scarlet, and in such a short time.

Weird.

But when all the pieces of their past were slotted into place, would she want to know about him or sharpen her boot to kick his behind?

They quickly ended the conversation; Owen still had hay bales to arrange before the party. Daniel left the faucet running in the hot tub and returned to the balcony.

"We need cowboy hats," he said, strolling out into the sunshine.

"We're going to a rodeo?"

"A bush dance at Owen's. There'll be lots of stomping and swinging and country music, and maybe later some AC/DC."

Holding an imaginary guitar, he let loose with a "Johnny Be Good" duckwalk across the balcony. He wondered which Scarlet would respond to his mini-performance...the adventure-loving woman he'd come to know these past days, or the far more restrained lady from D.C. with her classical tastes and restrained ways.

When her lips pressed together and her expression seemed to set, Daniel slowly straightened. Guess he had his answer. The re-emerging socialite was not amused, or didn't want to show that she was.

But then her expression ignited and once again she came alive. Skipping over, she caught his arm with hers and swung them both around and around in a classic square dance move. Laughing, relieved, he swept her up into the sling of his arms. Hearing her sandals land as she heeled them off along the way, he headed into the house and down the hall. Entering the bedroom, she blinked.

"Water's running," she said.

"Warm and deep and very soon sudsy."

In the bathroom, he set her down on the shaggy king-size mat laid out on the expansive tiled floor. Then he poured a mixture under the faucet. Bubbles foamed and the scent of lavender swirled out and all around.

"That looks incredibly relaxing." Stretching, pretending to yawn, she wound her hands and arms up through her hair and over her head. "I might just fall asleep."

"You can try."

He slipped her T-shirt up and off. Damn, he loved the fact she didn't wear a bra. In quick time, he peeled the jeans down her legs. As she kicked away the denim pooled around her feet, he ditched his own clothes. Then he took her hand and climbed into the spa.

As he found the ideal spot to settle against the elevated, padded headrest, she stepped in. He savored every movement as she edged carefully into the bubbling pool. Her calves disappeared beneath the surface, her upper legs. When she was submerged, he swirled her over and she straddled his lap. While his mouth made love to each breast in turn, she held his head and moved against him.

His arms slid up her back, holding her in place while their legs slipped over one another and his erection throbbed and grew. With her fingers twining through his hair, she nuzzled him while his tongue and teeth toyed with her nipples.

"You can do that all day," she murmured at the same time she slid an arm between them. Then her magic fingers began to work his engorged length up and down until he reached an inhuman, smoldering state. He wasn't sure what she was doing with her nails, but the combination of submerged slide and graze was going down very well. When she maneuvered herself a little higher, the tip of his erection trailed between the tops of her thighs and slid just a little inside her. Her hips moved as she held and steered him an inch higher, circling the head of his length around the most sensitive, responsive part of her. He groaned at the molten surge through his veins. His tongue rode around a tight nipple, then flicked it until she shuddered out a sigh and her neck rocked back. Knowing that she was using him to arouse herself more created an erotic image in his mind that had him throbbing, balanced on the edge. He wanted to enter her again, this time fully. He longed to grind her hips down while his ground unforgivably up.

But he didn't have protection. It was too difficult to use in the water. Not safe.

Easing her off, he stepped out of the hot tub, then helped her onto dry land, too. He grabbed two towels. After wrapping her in one and lashing the other around his hips, he carried her into the main suite and lowered her onto the bed. He took his sweet time wiping the beads of water and scented oil from her skin while she simply lay there, her gaze searching his face as she let him move this arm or that leg to get to all the interesting places.

By the time she was dry, the water had evaporated off his own steaming skin. He trailed his lips up the inside of her leg, stopping for a good long moment to open her folds and use his mouth to make sure she was as ready as he was. Then he found a condom.

Sheathed, he joined her again, kissing her deeply, showing her how much this meant.

How much *she* meant.

Her arms and legs wound around him as he positioned

himself between her opened thighs. Using as much restraint as he could muster, he thrust inside.

As he moved above her, his arm curled around her head. His focus on her dreamy expression and parted lips, he knew this time was different, even if he couldn't pinpoint why. Perhaps because they were in his home, because they'd been constant companions for days on end, mainly just the two of them.

Because he hadn't been with a woman anything like Scarlet before.

When the friction built and his climax slammed home with a force that rocked him, body and soul, he buried his face in the damp mantle of her hair and almost uttered the words. A phrase he hadn't said since he was a child. Riding the waves, feeling her contract and spasm as her own peak hit, he flinched at a stab of concern. A flash of insight.

Maybe he wasn't as in control as he'd thought.

Daniel had appropriate clothing and accessories brought in—hats, boots and chaps for him and a sexy black waistcoat for Scarlet.

When they arrived early at Owen's place, the music was already blaring. Daniel ignored the squeak, squeak of the CD's fiddle and ushered his beautiful date around the back of the house. The generous yard was decorated with hay bales and rustic plank fencing. Busy arranging a giant gum branch in front of a table filled with bush memorabilia, Owen had his back to them. When Daniel turned the music down, his foster dad swung around. Welcoming arms shot out.

"You snuck up on me!"

They gave each other a bear hug. "Need any help?"

Moving back, Owen dusted off his large hands. "All done."

Then he noticed Scarlet. Walking over with his easy stride, Owen offered her his hand. As they exchanged a few words about her time here, Daniel's stomach muscles twinged. His dad had met other women he'd dated but he'd never had this feeling before. Like he wanted them to meet again.

Another couple appeared, moving through the back gate into the yard. Owen greeted them, too, more introductions were made, drinks were poured. Only the soft stuff. Owen never drank, either, and his fundraising events were always alcohol-free. Then the music was turned up as more guests arrived.

"He's lovely," Scarlet said, tapping a boot to the music and looking around as the party lights blinked on.

"Don't know a person who wouldn't agree with you," he replied.

"You were lucky he asked to foster you."

She was looking at him as if to say, *I know about your father leaving, about your parents dying, but what happened in between?* His shoulders went back.

"Owen was a friend of the family. He offered to take me in." That's it.

"But what happened to your parents? I mean, you don't mind me asking, do you?"

He wanted to say, *Actually, yes, I do.*

"I don't talk about that part of my life."

"Never?" she asked.

"Ever," he replied.

Inside of twenty minutes, nearly a hundred people were chatting around the perimeter of the lawn dance floor or joining in the boot-scootin' fun. A small group had set up a barbecue. The aroma of sizzling sausages mixed with the scent of eucalypt. Everyone was in high spirits and in the mood to have fun.

Daniel caught up with people from the neighborhood he didn't see often enough. He kept Scarlet close and was certain to include her in conversations about sport meets from his school days and the antics they had gotten up to at blue light discos, the police-supervised dances for kids he'd attended when he was young. Daniel was pleased when a mate he'd known forever mentioned that his former teacher and mentor, Mr. Fielding, was doing well and visiting relatives in England. But no one brought up the connection—the trouble he'd got into as a teen and how Fielding had saved rebel Daniel McNeal from self-destructing.

In his last years in high school, he'd become angry. So full of rage, even now he couldn't put into words precisely why he'd suddenly wanted to put his fist through a wall, start arguments and be an ass to practically everyone, including poor Owen.

The day he'd stolen a car for a joyride—which had almost ended in his wiping out a couple at a pedestrian crossing— he'd expected to go to juvi. He was a ticking time bomb, certain he was going to turn out like his old man. He didn't deserve or even *want* anything from life.

But the car's owner—Mr. Fielding—had seen something golden in that tarnished boy. Behind the raging youth he'd perceived the child who'd suffered unspeakable tragedy and loss. Mr. Fielding had poured time into his student. Kept Daniel busy and focused around the clock. He'd shown endless patience teaching him everything he knew about the various realms of pure mathematics. At the end of that year, Daniel had found a purpose in life. At age nineteen, he'd started his business. Very soon thereafter, he'd made his first million. His first billion came a few years later.

As another song ended, Owen called out on the mic.

"You guys—Marco, Calum—get my son and his jillaroo on the floor, will you?"

Daniel didn't need to be pushed. He took Scarlet's plastic cup and set it on a nearby table.

"Let's do this," he said.

They moved to the bottom of a chain of couples. As in previous dances, his father gave instructions, this time for the heel-toe polka. After a couple of run-throughs, the music kicked in and the dance began in earnest. Everyone heel-toed, slid together, clapped and swung their partners around. Hooting and laughing ensued until the song finished and many were left out of breath, including Scarlet. Daniel caught her in his arms and swung her around again, high enough for her feet to lift off the ground.

"Want to go again?" he asked.

Sucking down a lungful of air, she nodded eagerly. But he caught something else shining in her eyes. Something different. The same apprehensive glimmer he'd noticed earlier that day.

With the applause dying, Owen announced, "Grab your partner for Ned Kelly's Last Dance!"

He and Scarlet joined in a group of ten couples who formed two columns. When the music began, Daniel moved in near his partner and bowed. He and Scarlet do-si-doed, then, coming together, bowed again. He swung Scarlet on his arm. Everyone clapped and stomped a foot while the lead couple swung around and around, then peeled away, gent down one side, lady down the other, all to the music's twanging beat.

When the lead couple circled around to the end of the line, the two joined hands and raised their arms to make an arch while, at the top of the line, couples continued to peel off, skipping down each side of the formation, then under the arch to reform the columns. The verse started over with a new lead couple—representing a groom and his bride—and the steps began all over again.

Enjoying themselves, he and Scarlet swung and skipped and danced around. When it was their turn at the lead—when they were meant to swing around and around while everyone else stopped and clapped—her boot heel slipped. Daniel caught and swooped her up and, barely missing a beat, he swung her around in his arms. When it was time for the next move, he set her down so he could peel off down one column of dancers while she headed down the other. A moment later, he joined her at the bottom of the formation, took her hands, raised their arms. And as the other nine couples joked and ducked beneath their arch, Daniel's gaze locked on hers and, in the slipstream of an instant, he felt his center shift.

While the music thumped and couples ducked, his fingers tightened, laced with hers. He was focused on the rhythm of the music, the squeak of the fiddle, the meaning behind this song. They were dancing, celebrating. He was the groom and Scarlet was the—

"The music's stopped," Scarlet said. "We can lower our arms now."

He did. But while the other couples congregated to hear instructions for the next dance, he brought her near, searched her face, her eyes. She was looking at him that way again. Well, if she had something to say, he wanted to hear it.

He led her off to a quiet spot behind a clump a melaleuca bushes. Then he asked her straight out. "What do you remember?"

"I remember I love jelly beans, but only the pink ones. I could eat them all day, but I limit myself. Or, at least, I try."

"What else?"

"My parents. My job. My friends, Cara Cranshaw, Francesca Orr, Lee, our receptionist at work. I remember Ariella's situation. I feel terrible having left her when she needed me."

"Do you remember us?" A beat passed before she nodded. "Everything?" She nodded again. He sucked down a breath. "How long?"

"Pretty much everything since before we left Hinchinbrook. The rest of it on the road trip."

His head went back. So she'd had her memory back when

they'd made love on the boat that last time. When they'd sped down that ocean road. Why the hell hadn't she told him before now? Had she set out to make him feel like a fool?

"So most of the time you were faking."

"Daniel, it wasn't like that. Please don't be angry."

"I'm Mr. Laid-back, remember? I don't do angry." Not anymore. Not like when he was a law-breaking kid.

"It's not as if I'm angry with you. I don't regret this trip, the things we've done. What we've shared."

"I know there's a 'but' coming."

Her eyes pleaded with his. "But it's time to get back."

"To mend your soiled reputation?"

"In your Waves posts, you never mentioned the name of the person you were traveling with. You never showed my face in any of the attachments."

"Yeah, well, I'm thoughtful like that. The best friend of the president's daughter can't be too careful."

Not that he or any member of the public knew that Ariella was Ted Morrow's daughter for sure.

"This has been fun. Unbelievably romantic and wild." She grazed a palm down his checked shirtfront. "But it's not me. Not really."

He remembered all the times they'd made love and cocked a wry brow. "Almost had me convinced."

"I was happy. I am…happy. But I have to go home to D.C. Daniel, I've remembered more about the past than I did before."

"What are you talking about?"

"I have a memory. It's always been there.… It's clearer now. More real. But whenever it comes, I feel as if I'm somehow standing outside of myself. It's hard to explain."

He'd stopped breathing. Blood clot? Psychosis? Good Lord.

He held her shoulders. "We need to get you to a doctor."

"What I need," she said, "are answers. And I know just where to get them."

Ten

"You were so brief on the phone," her mother said, lowering into the recliner where she routinely read fat novels while her husband played chess on his iPad. "Is everything all right?"

"Depends on how you look at it." Scarlet took a seat on the couch. "I have my memory back."

Sitting in his favorite chair, her father looked relieved. "So, you remember everything before that tumble?"

"Yes." Then she amended, "Up to a point."

Moments ago, when Faith Anders had opened the door of her home to her daughter and Daniel McNeal, Scarlet had fallen into her mother's outstretched arms, exhausted and relieved. Soon they were walking in here, to the same sitting room Scarlet now remembered so well. The big fireplace, that expensive artwork… When they passed the baby grand piano, she looked at it twice.

Her head hurt from going over fractured images and thoughts that kept on like a ticking clock in her brain. Either she was going mad or an event from her past was trying to tell her something she shouldn't ignore. Something she felt sure her parents could help her with.

"I'm up to date with my school days," Scarlet explained, "college, starting the business. I remember my friends and our relationships. I remember you both," she grinned "—of course. But I also remember...others."

Her mother's enthralled look changed to one of teasing concern. "You're sounding like a horror film. Are we about to hear that you can see ghosts?"

"In a way," Scarlet said, "I do see ghosts. And hear them. Sometimes I even smell them."

While her mother's face drained of color, her father reached across to set a consoling hand on his wife's arm.

"Scarlet, that's not funny. You're scaring your mother."

"I'm scared, too," she told him. "That's why I need to hear what you know."

Faith seemed to pale even more.

"When I was young," Scarlet went on, "I remember I had a friend. A girl who looked a lot like me. We used to play on a tire swing. A woman would watch over us and bring out lemonade."

Her father looked blindsided, as if someone had belted him over the back of his head with a rubber mallet.

His voice was a hoarse rasp. "How could you remember that far back?"

"You were only two years old," her mother said.

Scarlet withered in her seat. Her head began to tingle. She was right. But why did the memory seem so vital? Why wouldn't it leave her alone?

"That woman—she *was* real, wasn't she? They were *both* real." Scarlet tipped forward. "Who were they? Why were they so important that I need to remember them now?"

"All your life," her mother began, sounding drained, "we've debated whether or not to tell you."

Scarlet waited. And waited.

"Tell me *what?*"

"You had a sister…a twin." Closing his eyes, her father held the bridge of his nose. "Scarlet, she died."

Beside her, Daniel held her hand as the memories from long ago sharpened. But none of that made sense. A sister? *Who'd died?* But then, like a damaged movie reel with lines and glitches playing out in her mind, she remembered more.

That girl…

"She fell off the swing," Scarlet said, half to herself. "Hit her head." *Just like me.*

"She did fall," her father said. "And when she developed a fever, it was blamed on the accident. But she died of meningitis. We were devastated. Particularly your mother."

Scarlet brought herself back to the present. "Now that really doesn't make sense. This girl was my sister. My twin." She studied her mother's ashen face. "But in my mind you're not that girl's mother. That other woman…"

"That other woman you remember, Scarlet…" Her father took a deep breath. "She's your biological mother. We were married a year before you were born. After the accident, she was overcome with grief.…"

When he lowered his head, unable to go on, Scarlet looked to Faith and forced herself to ask the question that was stuck high in her throat.

"You're not my mother?"

Faith's eyes glistened with unshed tears. "I always tried to be the best mother I could be."

"Imogene…your mother…she blamed herself for not keeping a better eye on you both," her father said.

"But she *did* watch over us." Scarlet closed her eyes, and

the memory came back, sharper than ever. "In my mind, she's smiling, happy, always there."

"The day before the funeral," her father said, "we sent you away to stay with friends. The day after the ceremony, Imogene was gone. Just…vanished. I tried tracking her down. I succeeded a couple of times, but she refused to come home. Your mother…that is, *Faith,* was a good friend to the both of us. When I needed help, she was there. Before long, you started calling her Mommy. It might have been wrong, but we were grateful you didn't seem to be affected by any of it."

"So you let me forget," Scarlet said, feeling spacey. Feeling empty and betrayed.

"You were so innocent." Faith didn't wipe away the tear running down her face, leaving a line on her rouged cheek. "We'd planned to tell you when you got older, but we didn't want to upset your senior year, or disturb how well you were doing in college. Then you began building a career for yourself…" A defeated look came over her face. "I suppose we *all* wanted to forget."

Daniel spoke up. Though he was holding her hand, she'd almost forgotten he was there.

"Where's Imogene now?"

"I have no idea," her father said. "After she signed the divorce papers so that Faith and I could marry, I'm afraid we lost track."

Daniel had another question. "Where was she the last time you were in contact?"

Her father groaned. "Mexico."

When Scarlet's head drooped and her shoulders sagged, Daniel squeezed her hand tight.

"I promise you," he said, "we'll find her. We'll start looking right away."

Scarlet felt so deflated, so empty, she could barely muster the energy to speak.

"It's been twenty-five years," she said. "She's never once tried to find me. How does a mother do that to her child?"

Daniel brought his forehead to rest against hers. "I'm afraid you need to ask her that."

Eleven

Remarkable what some serious money could do.

After her parents' full disclosure two days ago, when Scarlet had learned the extraordinary truth behind her past, Daniel had promised to leave no rock unturned. They would find her mother, he'd vowed, and find her fast. Now, alighting from a chauffeur-driven limousine on this warm South Carolina day, Scarlet was only grateful that Daniel had access to the resources he did and that he was so willing to help.

After leaving her parents' home, they'd taken a beeline back to Daniel's penthouse where he'd made some well-placed calls. Within an hour, one of the East Coast's most successful private detectives was on the case, digging up records, searching for clues. The next twenty-four hours they'd played out an agonizing waiting game.

Food didn't interest her. Sleep wasn't happening. Waiting for news—*any* news—had reduced her to a bag of jangled nerves. All those years ago, she'd lost a mother *and* a sister...

a twin. How had her parents kept that dark, deluded secret all that time? She felt like the world's biggest fool. As if every moment she'd lived before now had been masked by a lie.

That realization made her feel even worse about keeping the truth from Daniel. She'd convinced herself that withholding the fact that her memory had returned was for the best. She hadn't wanted the adventure to end. When he'd confronted her at Owen's place that night—when the truth had finally come out—he'd looked so hurt. Whether her reasons were well-intentioned or not, she'd lied to him, just as her father and stepmother Faith had lied to her all these years.

As Daniel took her hand now and they headed down the path of this suburban home, Scarlet's thoughts went to Ariella and her predicament. Strange that within such a short amount of time, their situations should so closely echo each other. Both women wanted to find their birth mothers. Hopefully, today, Scarlet's search, at least, would be over.

This morning, the P.I. had supplied an address. Scarlet's mother, Imogene Anders, who now went by her maiden name of Barnes, lived inside this inconspicuous Myrtle Beach home. She'd neither remarried nor had more children. As she and Daniel reached a front door mottled with peeling green paint, Scarlet was gripped by excitement. Near crippled with anxiety. Happy but also still reeling with the knowledge of the awful set of events that had led to this point.

She had so many questions.

The P.I. had also provided the name and description of a woman who shared this house with Imogene. When the door opened, Scarlet guessed this must be Mrs. Rampling. Somewhere in her sixties, she was well-groomed, with salt-and-pepper hair and large gray-framed glasses that magnified small hazel eyes. Daniel introduced himself and Scarlet. The woman reciprocated by announcing, "I told that detective. This won't work."

Scarlet's hackles shot up. While Mrs. Rampling had acknowledged that Imogene Barnes did, in fact, reside here, she'd refused to answer any more of the P.I.'s questions. Neither would Imogene come to the door. Was her birth mother being held captive, or was she simply too cowardly to face the daughter she'd abandoned so many years ago?

"You know the situation." Scarlet pulled herself up tall. "Frankly, I'm not concerned about your opinion of whether this will work or whether it won't."

"What Scarlet means to say," Daniel cut in on a diplomatic note, "is that learning about her birth mother has been a shock. If you could pass on to Ms. Barnes that her daughter would appreciate a few minutes of her time, we'd be most grateful."

Mrs. Rampling played with the blue bandanna roped around her neck while she sized Scarlet up. "You don't look very strong."

Scarlet coughed. "What has that got to do with anything?"

"Just saying. You look as if you've had an easy life. Maybe some of this harder stuff is better left behind."

Scarlet's stomach roiled. Was that how Imogene had spoken about her family? That it was too hard to deal with? Was that what she'd told this Mrs. Rampling to pass on today?

"If Imogene has something to say," Scarlet said, steeling herself, "she ought to come out here and say it herself."

Mrs. Rampling's lips pursed more.

Scarlet wasn't devoid of sympathy. Confronting mistakes, accepting responsibilities, wasn't easy. Her recent time spent with Daniel had taught her that denying a situation's negatives was not only tempting, it could be downright addictive. To lose a child, of course, was on another level completely. That was a tragedy you'd want to forget if only you could. But Imogene Barnes had another child—one who'd been silenced for twenty-five years and deserved an audience now.

"Kindly tell Imogene that I'm here," Scarlet said. "Tell her I'm not leaving."

When Mrs. Rampling gave a sympathetic smile and began to close the door, Scarlet's threadbare patience snapped. She charged past the older woman and into the house. An instant later, she felt Daniel's fingertips brush her arm, a fraction short of holding her back. She could barely believe she was breaking the law, entering a private address without permission. But tough times called for tough measures.

The house smelled of overcooked cabbage. Paint on the walls had yellowed and the ceiling felt too low. If her mother hadn't left her behind, she might have grown up here. A far cry from the pomp of Georgetown.

"Imogene Barnes," she called out, feeling suddenly chilled and hugging herself. "This is your daughter. Scarlet." Hearing Daniel's footfalls behind her, not knowing what lay ahead, she edged farther down the hall. "Please. I want to speak with you."

A strong arm lashed around her waist—holding her back or steadying her? Because as stoic as she'd felt standing on that porch a second ago, now she was trembling, inside and out.

"I want her to say to my face she doesn't want to see me," she told Daniel. "I don't even need an explanation. But I deserve the courtesy of—"

Her words trailed off. Something shifting in an adjoining room had drawn her eye…a person sitting on a couch that faced an arched window. Only a rear view of the person's head was visible. The hair was an unusual color…a duller shade of her own golden red.

Entranced, Scarlet inched into the room while Mrs. Rampling voiced her objection.

"Don't stride right up," she said. "You'll frighten her."

Mrs. Rampling had it the wrong way around. Scarlet was the one who'd been a child, who must have been frightened when her mother hadn't come home. Not that Scarlet could recall much of that time other than living a normal life, having her father and Faith take care of her. Faith was the person who had brushed her hair in the mornings, who had listened to her enthusiastic attempts at playing the piano, who'd told her about boys and becoming a woman and if ever she had any questions—

Mrs. Rampling was clutching her arm. "Imogene doesn't know you," she said.

"And I don't know her." That's what she'd come to fix. "Imogene," Scarlet said clearly. *"Mother."*

She skirted around one end of the couch. Then stopped at the same time the woman with the faded red hair dragged her focus from the view out the window. Her eyes were green and bright. Or was that glassy? On hearing her daughter's voice— seeing her only living child in the flesh—her gaze didn't light with recognition. Didn't dim with shame. Her expression…

Well, it didn't change at all.

Scarlet sank onto her haunches.

That face was unknown yet so incredibly familiar. Scarlet felt as if she were looking into a crystal ball that foretold a time when she, too, would be skin and bone. Body ravaged. Mind blank.

Growing giddy, Scarlet let out a breath as Imogene turned back to the window.

"What happened?" she whispered.

Mrs. Rampling folded down on the couch next to her old friend. "Doctors call it early-onset Alzheimer's. Gets a handful of people as young as thirty. Their thoughts start to tangle. Little things at first…forgetting certain words, getting confused over everyday chores. As they get worse, they can feel like people are talking about them, accusing them.…" Mrs. Ramping folded a set of arthritic fingers over one of

Imogene's bony hands. "Most days now she doesn't remember me. Not a flicker."

"Did she ever tell you about her old life? Did she ever—" Scarlet swallowed at the bubble of emotion blocking her throat "—ever speak about her daughters?"

"She told me you were better off without her," Mrs. Rampling said. "At first I argued. She owed it to everyone, herself included, to get her tail back home and work the troubles out. But I think she knew way back, even then."

Dealing with that horrible accident, her sense of guilt… that would have been demanding enough without her thoughts being "tangled."

"And you've looked after her all these years?"

"She was a good friend," Mrs. Rampling said. "Helped me no end when my turd of a husband closed our accounts and tossed me out. Genie and I…we're like family."

Family? Scarlet took that word on board, let it settle in, then almost smiled.

She'd always remembered having a family. Now Scarlet was glad her mother had in some way enjoyed that kind of closeness too.

"It's hard," Mrs. Rampling went on, "when she's so confused that she starts to scream, then cry or even sob. She likes routine. Quiet. That's how I like to keep things, too." She sat back. "She did love you girls. If there's such a thing, I think she loved you *too* much."

Scarlet followed Imogene's sight line. The garden was awash with tulips. They reminded Scarlet of a field of raised pink jelly beans. In the middle of all the flowers stood a giant oak and, although Scarlet knew it wasn't really there—knew it wasn't real—she imagined the creak of a thick rope on a branch, then saw a tire swing swaying in the breeze and two little girls playing. She wanted to believe that her mother imagined that, too.

Her eyes misted with tears as Scarlet stumbled from the room, out of the house and into a shower of sunshine that provided no warmth. Daniel called after her. When he caught up and wrapped two strong arms around her, she leaned in and sucked back a lungful of air. All the long journey here, she'd vowed she wouldn't cry.

"It's okay, it's okay," Daniel said, rubbing her back.

"She doesn't remember me. Doesn't remember anything."

"You've done what you set out to do." He nuzzled her crown. "We'll go home."

"They must live on a shoestring. Mrs. Rampling...I wonder if she gets any help."

He held her tighter. "I'll write a check."

"No matter what happened in the past, Imogene...my mother deserves the best care. I know Dad would think so, too. She needs a full-time nurse. A good doctor."

"I'll look into it. Look after it."

She pressed her other wet cheek against his shirt. "She's so sick. God knows how much she suffered."

"I'll organize some funds. Some full-time care." With a crooked finger, he tipped her chin higher so that his tender gaze met hers. "You've coped with a lot these past few days. What do you say we get some rest?"

Scarlet frowned. He wanted them to leave. Already?

"I need to stay for a while. Make sure everything's organized."

"Okay. I'll book a hotel for a couple of days."

"It'll take more than that."

"A week?"

"I...I'm not sure."

She held her brow. Her thoughts were spinning. Her mother had abandoned her as a child but she could understand how that had come about, why Imogene's deteriorating condition might have played a part in her decision to stay away. Scarlet wished her father had tried harder to bring his wife home. That her mother had gotten some kind of help sooner. There was nothing she could do about that now. But she couldn't—wouldn't—abandon her mother now.

And then she remembered Faith, the woman who had cared for her, loved her all this time like a mother should. The person she'd called Mom could, at times, be haughty, controlling, constantly needing to remind people of their place in society, but she'd also always stuck by her family. For all her faults, Faith Anders had her heart in the right place.

Scarlet was certain she would understand her daughter's actions now.

"I've missed out on having Imogene in my life," Scarlet said. "She's missed out on having me. I want to stay with her, in that house, till I know I've done everything I can."

"Perhaps you'd better ask Mrs. Rampling before you move in." His wry grin eased and he took her hands. "Give yourself some time. Let a professional come in, size up the situation and give a report."

It made sense, she guessed. Her birth mother obviously needed a comprehensive evaluation and Scarlet had a job she'd neglected back in D.C. But she wanted to be there to help.

Then it came to her.

"She could come home with me!"

"Scarlet, this is her home. You heard her friend. She's comfortable in familiar surroundings. With people she knows."

"Mrs. Rampling could come, too. Or I could fund a vacation for her. She deserves a break."

"I don't think you understand what you're asking to take on."

"I'm her daughter."

"Honey, she doesn't know that."

Scarlet let go of his hands. He wasn't listening.

"I can't let you hand over some guilt money," she said, "then just walk away."

He rubbed his jaw, filed a hand back through his hair. Then he looked at the peeling green door. "I'm not sure what you want to happen here."

"I want to help her."

"She's *beyond* help. For God's sake, Scarlet, you can see that."

"You could do that to your mother? Walk away. Give up."

His gaze hardened, voice deepened. "We're not talking about me."

"Maybe if you didn't try to hide from your own past, you wouldn't feel this way about mine."

His smile was thin. "That won't work."

"So stop trying to talk me out of what I feel I have to do. I appreciate all you've done. But I have to do what I feel is right. This is my decision."

A strange, dark look shuttered the blue steel glinting in his eyes. "You've faced this. You needed to. But now you need to get on with your life. Stay in touch with what's going on here, but you can't let it eat you up."

"I can't let go of it, either."

"The alternative will tear you apart. It'll make you furious about stuff you can't change. About stuff that will screw with your head until you want to hit something. Anything."

He was speaking about himself, not her.

"It doesn't have to be like that. If I bring her home, get some specialists in, take some time off work—"

"Fine." Throwing up his hands, his face dark, he backed away. "Your life. Your choice."

She wanted to shout, *I don't have a choice.*

"So what are you going to do now?" he asked.

"Now?"

"As in this minute now?"

"I'm going to go back inside, speak to Mrs. Rampling. Explain what I have in mind. Why I think it's important."

"And if she says no?"

"There are always the courts."

"Fun," he muttered.

"I'm doing this." *No matter what you say.*

"Then you'll do it without me." He cast a glance over at the limo. "I'll find a cab and leave the car. You'll need it. Let me know when you want to fly home and I'll arrange for the jet to pick you up."

Her eyes were stinging. Why couldn't he try to understand? Step out of his own reality and see her point? Understand her needs? Life wasn't all about running away.

"I can organize my own transport," she got out.

"If that's the way you want it."

She swallowed. "That's what I want."

He looked at her for a long tense moment. When his jutting jaw relaxed, she thought he was going to apologize, hold her, kiss her. But he only exhaled and, shaking his head, walked away.

Twelve

"How is she settling in?"

Descending the stairs of her two-bedroom Georgetown town house, Scarlet hesitated at her stepmother's question. Faith was visiting her daughter for the second time since Scarlet had brought Imogene back here from Myrtle Beach. As to answering that question: how was she settling in? Scarlet wasn't certain how to respond. Having her biological mother stay with her was an idea spawned with the very best of intentions. Talking Mrs. Rampling into it had been difficult. The elderly woman had eventually sat back and studied her friend and decided that, if Imogene had retained any of her memory, at this stage in her life she'd probably *want* to go with her daughter. But she'd insisted on coming along, staying in D.C., too. In hindsight, Scarlet was nothing short of grateful.

Rather than a hospital stay, a health team had been brought in to assess Imogene. But even the full-time nurse had a hard time when Imogene suddenly went off. Poor woman. Imogene was so thin and worn. It didn't look as if she had enough strength to move an arm let alone have an outburst.

Faith was sitting behind the piano. Drawing nearer, Scarlet explained.

"Mrs. Rampling assures me she's doing fine. The nurse says she'll need to be tube-fed soon. She recommended full-time care at a facility that specializes in this kind of patient."

Faith was looking absently at the piano keys. She played a few chords of a lilting melody that Scarlet recognized. Something she used to know many years ago. But Scarlet didn't want to play. She only wanted all the bad feelings to go away. She'd wanted answers but in finding those she'd simply created more questions.

"What do I do?" she asked. "The nurse wants Imogene in a home, Mrs. Rampling is waiting patiently to return her friend to Myrtle Beach and I'm responsible for this mess."

Faith played a few more chords. The tinkling, the safe memories of that music, made Scarlet feel less lost. She rested her fingers on the keys. Their smooth cool surface made her relax.

"You understand that what happened all those years ago wasn't in any way your fault," Faith said. "If you knew her, before that horrible day…Imogene was so optimistic about life. Generous. Funny. She wouldn't want you to feel responsible for her now."

Scarlet felt torn. Sad for the loss, happy that she'd known that other younger Imogene once, if only for a brief time.

Sighing, she joined in playing the melody.

"She was a good mother," Scarlet finally said, certain of it.

"Talented, too. When you first began to jump behind the piano, we knew you inherited that gift from her. I can play but Imogene was brilliant."

"I haven't really played in years."

"You should start again. Play some old favorites." Faith sent over a warm smile. "Find some new tunes, too."

They'd spoken again about the events that followed that tragic accident years ago. Faith and her father had shown Scarlet photos and accompanied her when she'd asked to see her sister's grave. Her twin's name was Laura.

Since discovering the truth, Scarlet's sense of betrayal had faded. When she'd had time to have it all sink in, she understood how the situation had come about. The news had been devastating to hear as an adult. Courage is one thing, but at what age could they have told a little girl she'd lost so much?

Of course, she'd gained something, too. A second mother who, despite her faults, had done her best to try to protect her daughter. Scarlet wondered what kind of relationship she might one day have with her own children. Although, since that argument with Daniel, she couldn't imagine herself ever walking down an aisle or even having a family, particularly since doctors had suggested there was a chance that Imogene's disease could be passed down to her.

The only times she and Daniel had spoken had been a couple of clipped phone calls. As the days dragged on, however, so many times she had almost surrendered and dialed his number. She missed him more than she'd ever thought possible. Lying awake at night, she remembered his laugh, how his strong arms had felt wrapped around her. She missed their conversations and adventures. She ached to have him look into her eyes and tell her again how much she meant to him.

But Daniel McNeal was the original Mr. Good Time. His world revolved around entertainment and fun. Sometimes she wondered where he found the time to manage a hugely successful company. Everything about Daniel seemed so effortless. So addictive.

Still, whenever that sinking lonely feeling threatened to engulf her, she reminded herself that he was probably over their affair by now. She'd provided a diversion, but in these circumstances he wouldn't want to continue seeing her. Or not for long. Hadn't he made that clear? Her world was too full of constraints and boring protocol and responsibilities. The real Scarlet was back and she'd known all along, on scores that truly counted, she and Daniel McNeal simply weren't compatible.

She only hoped it didn't take a lifetime to convince her heart of that.

"It must have been hard for you and Dad to have kept those secrets for so long," Scarlet said.

"We didn't want to risk you growing up thinking you weren't loved. Because you were, and are, very much. Sometimes, when we're very close to a situation…to a person…it's difficult to know what's best."

Scarlet looked across and caught Faith's smile, soft and understanding. Perhaps she wasn't the only one who had grown and changed these past weeks. This moment she felt close to Faith, her mother, in a way she never had before.

Scarlet played along with Faith on the piano until they came to the end of the song. Then they turned to each other and hugged. Long and strong. An embrace that said they'd be there for each other no matter what. Mother to daughter, daughter to mom.

"I always felt privileged to have brought you up," Faith said, drawing away. "I wanted to give you so much, smother you with love, make sure you were safe. Taken care of. I admit, there were times I went too far."

Like making her concerns about Daniel known at that black-tie event. She and Daniel would meet again at Cara and Max's wedding. Would he treat her with disdain? Sweep her up into his arms and carry her away? More likely he'd bring a date. Scarlet's stomach swooped. On top of everything else, she didn't know if she could handle that.

Scarlet closed the piano lid.

Her mother's hand came to rest over hers. "I don't have to tell you I was pleased when you started seeing Everett. I thought I needed to have you settled, well matched. I'd convinced myself that of course you were happy."

"I bumped into Everett the other day. I was about to do the polite thing, say hello. He only gave me a cold, blank look, as if I didn't exist."

Her mother's face crumpled. "Oh, darling, I'm sorry."

She didn't want her mom to feel bad. Lots of mothers wanted to play matchmaker for their daughters. She saw the end product all the time when she was asked to organize weddings where the mother looked more pleased about the union than the daughter did. That would have been her and Everett. Well, she was certain she'd never make that kind of mistake again.

Faith brushed a sweep of hair away from Scarlet's cheek. "I like your hair loose," she said.

Scarlet was about to say, *So does Daniel.* Instead, she simply said, "Thanks."

Faith lowered her chin. "Have you heard from Daniel since Myrtle Beach?"

Faith knew about the argument, how upset her daughter had been.

"We've spoken briefly on the phone," Scarlet said. "He said he was sorry we quarreled."

"But you didn't accept his apology?"

"Daniel McNeal is all about staying free and easy. He lives on a cloud."

"I admit that his reputation did nothing to ingratiate me toward him. Posing nude for a calendar… Is he still going to do that?"

"I'm not sure." If he did, they'd sell a million, particularly with that butterfly tattoo in a place the public wouldn't normally see.

"It is for a good cause, I suppose…" Faith sighed. "Thing is, after seeing how close you two had grown…after seeing the way he looked at you when you came back from your trip… Frankly, I've changed my mind. I believe he truly cares about you."

Scarlet swallowed down the rising emotion, the longing that things could be different. "He'll find someone else."

A string of them.

"Wouldn't it be wonderful if we could make everyone we loved happy a hundred per cent of the time?"

Scarlet studied her mother's knowing look. And she had to admit—it was true. Although she wished she didn't, she *did* love Daniel, and she wished she could make him happy. But after seeing his face, how he reacted at Myrtle Beach, that was never going to happen. He had his priorities and she had hers. This parting might hurt worse than a knife through the heart but in the end it was better they were finished. She only wished she never had to face him again, and so soon.

She'd been away from the office, the duties and friends she loved this long. Early the next morning, Scarlet arrived at DC Affairs and headed straight for Ariella's office.

"It's so good to have you back," Ariella said as Scarlet crossed over to her friend's desk and they hugged. "From your texts, I get the sense a lot has been going on."

Scarlet filled her friend in on the details of her impromptu trip to Australia. Ariella sighed when she heard about the beaches and koalas. Scarlet passed on how her memory had returned in full. Finally she spoke about those very old memories and tracking down Imogene, bringing her home.

Of course, being one of the dearest friends she had, Ariella understood perfectly.

"And Daniel McNeal?" she asked.

"Out of the picture."

"Well, that was short but, I'm sure, incredibly sweet."

"He's not known for his long relationships. Thankfully our affair didn't hit any headlines. I didn't want any whiff of a scandal affecting business here," she said stoically, pacing the room.

"I for one think the whole thing wildly romantic. And given romance is a big part of the name of our game at DC Affairs, who knows. A few leaks might have done us good."

Scarlet grinned. She hadn't thought of it that way.

"Speaking of leaks…I heard the news on the radio coming in."

"About the congressional commission that's been formed to crack open the hacking scandal?"

"That, too."

ANS's excuse about having spoken with a housekeeper in uncovering the paternity story hadn't held water. Leaks and wiretaps had been unearthed all over the place. Email accounts had been hacked. Authorities were determined to get to, and punish, the people who had ordered the eavesdropping and broken the law. The commission had allegedly received audio evidence that confirmed ANS reporters Troy Hall and Brandon Ames plotted to hire hackers to record phone and computer activity of certain relatives of Eleanor Albert— Ariella's birth mother—and old friends in Fields, Montana, where the president and his high school sweetheart had grown up. Charges were pending.

Daniel's name had also been mentioned as being one of the experts who would be called up to testify. He wouldn't be happy about that. But Ariella must have been grateful—in one way at least—that someone had broken the law and dug into the president's past.

"So I guess the entire world knows now," Scarlet said.

The press had gone wild. Everyone wanted to know whether there was any truth in Ted Morrow's claim that he hadn't a clue he was a father.

"I won't give an interview. But, yes. It's official. President Morrow is Ariella Winthrop's biological dad." A small smile curved Ariella's lips. "We've spoken on the phone. He wants to meet me."

"Well, of course he does!"

"I have so many questions."

"I know the feeling."

"There's so much time to make up for."

"And it's only a matter of time before they find your biological mom."

"Even if she doesn't want to be found. Maybe I'd be better off if they didn't find her," Ariella muttered at her desktop, then shot a concerned look up at Scarlet. "I didn't mean—"

That perhaps Scarlet would've been better off not finding Imogene? "I know you didn't," Scarlet assured her friend.

Ariella was moving out from behind her desk. "And here we were a few months ago thinking we had uncomplicated lives."

They met in the middle of the room and, facing each other, held hands.

Ariella said, "I don't know what I'd do without my friends."

From her heart, Scarlet replied, "You'll never have to find out."

Thirteen

Scowling, Daniel peddled harder. "I'm not calling her again."

Morgan arched a brow. "Probably wise."

"She can get all cut up about what happened in her past, she can blow off about it all she wants." Daniel stepped up the speed on his state-of-the-art exercise bike from high to pretty-much-dying-here. "But I don't have to stick around," he panted, "and watch her hit the rocks."

"Absolutely. Your Scarlet can navigate her own life."

"She's not *my* Scarlet." He stopped peddling. "And why do I get the impression you're not on my side?"

"Would I be here if I wasn't?" Morgan moved to the treadmill next to his exercise bike and ran a finger over the arm. "It's just… Well, I like her."

"Me, too. Even if she drives me nuts." He started peddling like crazy again. "When she finally told me that she'd had her memory back most of the time we were in Australia, I was upset. I felt like a fool but I let it slide. Back here, she wanted to find her biological mother, so I pulled out all the stops and got the best P.I. I could on the case. When he'd tracked that poor woman down, I flew Scarlet to South Carolina, no problem. But I'll tell you something. It's no fun watching a female get that distressed. Seeing her cry." His chest hurt so much, he thought he was having a coronary, and not from the exercise. "Meeting her real mother again after so long…seeing her like that. Scarlet was devastated. I don't blame her." He eased up on the speed. "Thing is, what she's doing now is wrong."

"In your opinion."

Morgan put down her *Investor's Business Daily* to recalibrate the treadmill's electronic display board.

"I think things through," he said. "I determine outcomes. Make foolproof plans. To summarize, I'm rarely wrong."

"Rarely."

"Your point?"

"You're not right. You hurt her deeply. Go over and apologize."

"I already *have*. On the phone. Three times."

"On the phone."

"I tell her I'm sorry. She says good, thank you and hangs up. I say, I miss you. She says good and hangs up."

"What did you say the third time?"

"I groveled. Big-time. She didn't seem to believe me."

"Why do you think that?"

"She hung up."

"I'd have changed my number by now." She swung up onto the treadmill track. "Do it again," she said. "Do it in person and make it stick. In case you hadn't noticed, you're in love with that woman."

He stopped dead. Considered. Morgan was intuitive….

"Do you think it's possible?"

"There's still talk we'll colonize Mars." Morgan set off on a jog. "You're not a young man anymore."

Grabbing his hand towel, he wiped the sweat pouring from his face, his chest. "I'm not *that* old."

"If you want to wait, I suppose…" She jogged faster. "But don't complain if she gets away."

"You're talking about falling down on one knee. Wedding bells." He threw his towel at the wall. *"Marriage."*

"Imagine the delightful guests." Now she was running with the grace and speed of a gazelle. "Don't forget a good band and accommodation should be provided."

He didn't crack a smile.

"What if I'm not cut out for a wife and kids?"

"You know the song. 'Ev-erybody needs some-bod-y to love.'"

"Scarlet mentioned during that last call…" His voice lowered. "She's worried that she might have inherited a predisposition to her mother's disease."

"It's possible." Morgan looked at him hard. "Would that matter to you?"

"You know it wouldn't. I just didn't know what to say. How to reassure her."

"Something for your homework book."

"What about you?" he asked. "Any love interests I should know about?"

"I'm looking at scheduling a regular love life into my planner one of these years."

"When you meet Mr. Right, I want an invite to the wedding."

"You'd have to give me time off for that."

"You're right. I'm a slave driver. Take a month off starting now. Take two."

She jumped and left the tread flying. "I was looking at trekking through Italy. But it'd cost you a fortune."

After Morgan left the penthouse gym and returned to her own suite, Daniel sat on the balcony until sunset, looking out at the capital. He went over his argument with Scarlet again, too many times to count. And then he went farther back.

Although he cringed, he forced his mind to pin down events of that fateful night so long ago. He went through every detail—sights, sounds, smells, anger, fear. Finally dread. When he'd played the scene through to the end, he rewound to the beginning and went over it again.

They'd said it was murder.

A couple of months after his mother had kicked her husband out, Daniel's father hit rock bottom. Drunk as a skunk, not a penny to his name, he showed up on the front landing of the family home. While he'd bashed on the door, called out slurred abuse, Daniel and his mum had huddled inside, praying that he'd leave or the neighbors would call the police. They couldn't make the call themselves. The bill hadn't been paid for a year. As his father had railed on, Daniel covered his ears, tried to be brave, but soon he'd begun to cry.

His mother, however, stayed strong, wiping her son's tears, holding him close. Finally she opened the door and told her husband—pleaded with him—to change for his family's sake, for his son. She'd admitted they were ashamed of him, and it was true. Daniel couldn't bring himself to look his father in the eye anymore.

When his father insulted her again, his mother said he could rot in hell. That's when his dad got mad. The kind of mad that dims a man's gaze with a bloodred fog. He'd growled that this was *his* house. No one was pushing him out. He was coming in and she'd better not try to stop him.

Daniel was only five at the time but he knew he had to run, get help. He was headed out the back door when he heard the screams, his mother's, then his father's. He found his father standing on the front landing, swaying, holding on to the rail and looking down. Then he kind of disintegrated, like a bag of sand split down the middle. Shaking, Daniel peered down the stairs to the scene below.

His mother lay on that square of concrete, broken. Still.

His father had committed suicide two weeks later.

In adulthood, Daniel had got hold of the police report relating to his mother's accident. Right leg fracture. Fifth and sixth vertebrae shattered. Spinal cord snapped. He'd never spoken of that night. Not to anyone, not even Owen. What good did it do to remember? Whenever an image sneaked into the corners of his mind, he wanted to hit something. Wanted to beat it down. Change it back.

If he could, he'd destroy those memories before they had a chance to destroy him.

But he'd come to understand. A person couldn't always keep something like that locked away, hidden inside, without it manifesting itself in other ways.

Around midnight, Daniel found his feet and, exhausted, moved inside to brew coffee. Then, with a steaming full mug, he camped out on the couch and willed himself to take his memories farther back still. Finally he had a vision of his father, younger, smiling, singing. Even dancing. The family had plenty of food on the table and no one argued over unpaid bills. His life was easy, carefree, like a kid's life ought to be. Whenever his dad stopped to kick a ball or ruffle his hair, Daniel had seen a superhero. A role model for the kind of man he wanted to be someday. Before things had turned rotten, there'd been good times. Lots of them.

He'd forgotten.

His jaw clenched. Hands, too. But he couldn't rid himself of the urge. Perhaps in the back of his mind, he'd known this day would come.

Tucked way on a wardrobe shelf in one of the spare rooms, he found it, packed in a brown cardboard box. Years before he'd brought the box over with him from Australia. He couldn't bear to think of it being stored in his primary home. Nor could he find the wherewithal to toss it away.

Settling the box on the floor, he knelt, tried to clear his head and opened the lid.

The wood of the fiddle was dark and smooth. The smell was old. Forgotten. When he scooped the fiddle up, leveled the instrument at his chin like his father had taught him to do, his fingers began to tingle. Inhaling the rich wood scent, closing his eyes, he let himself go back. Allowed himself to feel.

In his mind, his father was laughing, standing tapping his foot as friends who had gathered for the night clapped and danced. His mother was there and Daniel smiled, remembering that look on her face, the shine in her eyes and the admiring curve of her mouth.

She'd loved her husband. And he'd loved her. So deeply that people only had to see them together to know it was true. Their bond hadn't needed words to describe it or a theory to explain it. It simply was. The way love was supposed to be.

Daniel opened his eyes.

And thought of Scarlet.

Fourteen

When Scarlet spied Daniel entering the reception ballroom, she told her stupid heart to stop thumping. Then, with suddenly shaky hands, she resumed smoothing one of the guest chair's dress bows. With Cara and Max's wedding due to start here at this highly sought-after venue in thirty minutes, she didn't need distractions, particularly the kind this man routinely tossed her way.

"Thanks," she called across the vacant room, "but I have everything under control. No need for you to be back here."

When Daniel didn't slow his advance, Scarlet tore her gaze from the mesmerizing roll of broad shoulders housed beneath that impeccably fitted dinner jacket and, straightening to her full height, showed him her back. She couldn't be clearer than that.

"I'm not here to talk about the wedding," he said.

"Well, that's all I'm focused on at the moment." She walked a resolute line to the next table. "If you'll excuse me…"

Her stomach was knotted all the way up to her throat. But if there'd ever been a day she needed to keep it together, this was it. Cara would soon be making her big trip down the aisle. She and Max were so well suited, so in love, Scarlet couldn't be more pleased for them both. But she'd be lying to deny that sharing in this time left her wondering all the more about her own future.

During her stay with Daniel in Australia, their issues had evaporated into so much steam. They'd found a common space to share, to live, to be wildly blissfully happy. But everyone had to return to reality sometime and Daniel's was a bitter place to dwell. While he gave off an easygoing, carefree air, at his core lived a boy who had stomped on and buried his past.

How Daniel handled his affairs was his business. But Scarlet had chosen a different path. Even when the hurt of looking back was nearly unbearable, she'd taken steps to heal. To thrive, she needed to forgive, embrace and move on. Unfortunately, Daniel didn't see things in quite the same way.

As she moved to straighten another bow, his deep voice reached out to touch her from behind.

"This all looks great, what you've done for the ceremony, in here and outside. Max and Cara will walk away with a lot of memories."

"All good, I hope."

"Earlier this week I took a tour of this place," he went on.

Fixing the daisies in a floral centerpiece, Scarlet paused. She wasn't nearly as starchy and uptight as she'd been a few weeks ago. Still she took pride in making certain all her events ran smoothly. No last-minute changes. No jack-in-the-box surprises. She rotated to face him.

"You came here earlier with Max?" she asked carefully.

"I came alone." Rethinking that, he tugged an ear. "That's

not entirely true. I came with a gang of ghosts dragging on my heels."

She returned to the centerpiece.

"I don't blame you," he said, "for not wanting to speak with me now. I didn't listen when you needed me to. I didn't know how."

A crippling ache released in her chest. That's right. He *hadn't* listened and in that moment when they'd quarreled she'd never felt more invalidated. He might choose to hide behind a lead-lined wall. Scarlet did not.

Out of the corner of her eye, she saw his long legs in pressed black trousers come closer and the nerves kicking around in her stomach went into overdrive.

"How's your mother, Imogene, doing?" he asked.

"Her illness…" Scarlet swallowed against the lump in her throat. "She needs full-time care."

"Must be difficult."

Difficult? She turned to face him.

"If you want to know, seeing her like this breaks my heart. I'll never know my real mother and now she'll never know me again." She drew up tall, crossed her arms. "But I'm done feeling sorry for myself. I'm trying to accept the past—in fact, I've embraced it despite your advice."

As a pulse beat high in his cheek, he ran a hand through his hair, leaving a trail of dark blond spikes.

"It was bad advice," he admitted.

She uncrossed her arms. She supposed he deserved to hear the rest. That he hadn't been entirely wrong.

"Mrs. Rampling, the doctor and I have spoken at great length. We've decided that Imogene ought to go back to Carolina. To the home they both know. I'll find a full-time nurse to help down there, and I'll visit as often as I can."

"Build some new memories." He sauntered closer. "You know I have some memories of my own. Good ones, I mean."

She was curious. "Of when you were young?"

"Of my father laughing and helping his neighbors, his friends. Of him swinging me over his shoulder so we could hurry in from the shed and be on time for tea. Lately I've thought about those times a lot." His blue gaze glistened. "I'm a slow teach but it finally sank in. *That's* the stuff I need to hold on to and remember. The good parts. The happy times."

Scarlet studied him hard. Had he truly accepted all the loss and frustration from his childhood? She wasn't sure she believed it. But if she were wrong and he had become friends with the past—with that part of himself—then hats off. Either way, Daniel would continue on his own path, as would she. And Scarlet wished them both luck. More challenges lay ahead. For better or worse, that was life.

Daniel shucked back those big shoulders of his. "Can you spare a minute? I have something I'd like to show you."

"Sorry. No time."

Scarlet might be ahead of schedule but going off with Daniel anywhere, for any reason, simply was not smart. He was too distracting, particularly looking so unusually humble.

"Two minutes," he said.

"I'm sorry but—"

Before she finished, he'd taken her hand. Those strong warm fingers folded around hers and her icy shell thawed enough to allow in a thin shard of maybe. Scarlet wouldn't change her mind about dating him again, if that's what he was after; she and Daniel could never go back. Frankly, she'd have a hard time with them being anything close to friends, even for Cara and Max's sake. Simply to look at him and remember hurt too much.

But she didn't wish him any ill will. And if life was about growing, he'd given her more to sow in these past weeks than anyone who had ever come before. He'd made a huge difference in how she viewed relationships. Saw herself. For that she was grateful.

She pulled her hand away and, after a torn moment, feeling strong enough, she followed him out.

When he fanned open the door to an adjoining room in this usually fully booked venue, a different world seemed to leap out at her. Photos were positioned *everywhere*. Lots were blown up to various sizes. Others remained in their original state. They hung on the walls, were mounted on easels, dangled from the ceiling on ribbon or twine. The majority were in color but more than a few captured a timeless moment in poignant black and white. Each snap was from the past, either Daniel's or her own.

Dazed—*amazed*—Scarlet edged inside.

The shot directly in front of her portrayed Scarlet as a tot, wearing a white pinafore and sitting on her father's knee while he read *Goldilocks* from a gold-leafed storybook. Turning around, she saw Daniel as a toddler dressed in worn shorts and a football team's T-shirt. His cheeks big, he blew bubbles with a woman who had the same fair hair and laughing blue eyes. Moving on, Scarlet and her twin stood on the front seat of a brand-new green sedan while her biological mother fooled around, pretending to steer the stationary car. A memory trace lit, igniting flashes on a runaway fuse, and suddenly she could smell that fresh seat leather. Again she was inhaling her mother's sweet perfume.

Further on, a four- or five-year-old Daniel hugged his mom and dad in the scrubby backyard of a suburban weatherboard home. Beside that photo, on a battered stool, lay a violin that looked a hundred years old. Scarlet thought back. Who did that instrument belong to? Had Daniel ever played as a boy? Not likely. He enjoyed rock—the heavier, the better.

To her right was perhaps the largest, most poignant picture of all. In the background, stood her birth mother, looking so proud and healthy as she smiled over at her daughters. In a foreground filled with tulips, Scarlet tried to push her laughing twin in the tire swing, a haunting scene which lay half-pieced-together in her mind like snippets from a beautiful dream. All of it was gone save for memories, this picture and the bittersweet ache that now threatened to engulf her.

Her breathing had grown choppy. Every inch, inside and out, felt insufferably weak, yet also warm and infinitely humbled. When she tried to speak, her words came out a choked whisper.

"Where did you get these?"

Daniel stood directly behind her. "From albums and yellowed envelopes and shoeboxes tied with string. Your mother, Faith, helped."

Given how she'd changed her opinion of him, Scarlet could believe it.

"What about that violin?" She nodded across at it.

"A fiddle."

"Is it yours?"

"Yep." He smiled softly. "It's mine."

Then he did the most amazing thing. Daniel told her a story from his childhood, a sad and violent tale that left Scarlet's eyes edged with tears. When he'd finished, looking remarkably composed—relieved—he nodded to her left.

A few feet from the stool stood a lacquered white dresser. On its ledge lay an armful of pink tulips and an enormous bowl filled with matching jelly beans. Scarlet swallowed back tears. He'd thought of everything.

Daniel had moved to stand beside her. As his body heat radiated out and seeped in, she watched his calm, knowing gaze sweep the room.

"A stone will always sink in my chest whenever I think of my father losing his job, reaching for a bottle that was his 'one too many.' But I can look at these moments and admit...I'm grateful for that very early time. For the family I once had." His jaw shifted as he paused. "I'd give anything to have it back."

A hot tear dropped down her cheek. Daniel could be patronizing, facetious, but with all her heart she believed him now. This wasn't some cheap trick. He'd finally accepted the cards fate had dealt and, from Scarlet's perspective, that acceptance came as a double shock. Five minutes ago, she'd thought *she* was streets ahead in the self-healing stakes.

When he searched her eyes with an openness that bared his soul, she read his mind and took two steps back.

"Look, this is all incredibly touching. I admit. I'm moved. But, Daniel—"

"I'm in love with you," he said, and her mind froze, then flooded with stunned disbelief. She studied him with a sidelong glance.

"What did you say?"

"I love you," he said again as his gaze roamed her face. "The kind of love that never goes away, that keeps getting stronger every hour, every day."

Blindsided, she shook her head. Daniel didn't go for that kind of complication. He didn't want the hassle. The routine. She'd believed that was part of the reason he'd pushed her away and had left her that day. You couldn't lose something you'd never had.

"You're confused," she decided.

"I'm crystal clear," he replied. "I want to wake every morning knowing that you're curled up beside me. I'm committed to whatever life throws our way." His head slanted and he cupped her cheek with a big, warm palm. "I'm sure, no matter where this journey takes me, I'll never give up hoping that one day, somehow, you'll love me, too."

Even as her heart gave a kick, she narrowed her eyes. A

silly part of her almost wanted to believe but, honestly, this was all a little transparent.

"You want us to be lovers again." He wanted her in his bed.

"Yes, I want us to be lovers. *And* friends. Best friends."

"Best friends can't feel the way I feel about you. Whenever I'm with you, the things that you do, it's like trying to stand up in a whirlwind. Whenever you're around I'm tossed up." She cast a clarifying glance around. "Completely thrown off balance."

His arm coiled around her waist and he brought her close. "You mean like this?"

There should have been a moment of hesitation. An instant where she pushed against his chest and told him to back off. At least to slow down. Instead, as his other arm wound around her upper back and his head lowered over hers, she found herself going limp, welcoming surrender and relishing the split second before his mouth captured hers.

When their lips touched, she felt only the thrill of wonder and a blinding inner peace. Then he drew her closer still, the hard planes of his chest pressed against her breasts, and she simply melted more. With her palm finding his jaw, he deepened the kiss until she ran out of air and all her jumbled world settled and joined seamlessly with his.

After he slowly broke away, he dropped a lingering kiss on her cheek, on her ear. He was breathing deeply. For the life of her, she couldn't think straight. Figure out what to do next.

She'd forgiven her childhood past. Could she possibly find it in her heart to forgive Daniel, too? This contact—his strength and skill and tenderness… Despite having lived in separate worlds, were two people simply meant to be?

Leaning back in the circle of his arms, she pressed a palm to her brow.

"I'm spinning again," she said.

A finger tilted her chin up and his gaze meshed with hers.

"This is just a theory, but ever consider the possibility that you might feel the same way about me? That you're in love, too?"

Letting out her breath, she surrendered the truth. "I *know* I'm in love with you." She frowned. "Maybe because you're so bad for me."

"Now tell me. Does this feel bad?"

Then he kissed her again, and this time the entire room became a swooping carnival ride. As he held and curled over her, she dissolved, utterly undone. When he finally released her, she was stripped bare. Dizzy and defenseless.

"I love you," she admitted again, and was half-okay saying it this time.

"And when I ask you to marry me, you might even say yes."

Her knees went but with two powerful arms locked around her, she didn't slide. Although hyperventilation was on the cards.

"You're proposing?" she got out.

"I want a family. Our family. A boy I can teach how to fish and kick three kinds of ball. A girl to spoil with frilly frocks and stories about magic ponies."

A tear fell from the outside corner of one eye, curling around and tickling her chin. If this was a dream, she'd gladly sleep forever.

"You want that with me?" She thought again about her mother's problem, about whether she might one day turn out the same way.

"Scarlet, I don't want to be with anyone but you from this moment till the day I die. Doesn't matter where or how, I want to spend our lives together, whatever comes our way."

More tears fell. Her throat was thick with disbelief. With overwhelming love. She sobbed out a clipped laugh.

"You really are a romantic, aren't you?"

"Guess what?" The tip of his nose circled hers. "So are you."

Their lips met and she melted into another mindless kiss. But when they surfaced again sometime later, Scarlet winced at a jab of guilt.

"There's a wedding due to start."

He showed no sign of releasing her. "We could ask the minister to make it a double service? That'd be a nice surprise."

"*Daniel*. That wouldn't be right."

He blinked, cocked his head. "No, no. Of course not."

Winding her arms around his neck, she arched a brow. "I was thinking more a ceremony on a deserted beach at sundown with your motorcycle parked close by for a speedy escape."

His eyes brimmed with laughter. His face filled with love. Coming close to kiss her again, the man she would adore forever openly confessed, "That sounds like pure heaven to me."

* * * * *

REQUEST YOUR FREE BOOKS!

2 FREE NOVELS PLUS 2 FREE GIFTS!

HARLEQUIN®

Desire

ALWAYS POWERFUL, PASSIONATE AND PROVOCATIVE

YES! Please send me 2 FREE Harlequin Desire® novels and my 2 FREE gifts (gifts are worth about $10). After receiving them, if I don't wish to receive any more books, I can return the shipping statement marked "cancel." If I don't cancel, I will receive 6 brand-new novels every month and be billed just $4.30 per book in the U.S. or $4.99 per book in Canada. That's a savings of at least 14% off the cover price! It's quite a bargain! Shipping and handling is just 50¢ per book in the U.S. and 75¢ per book in Canada.* I understand that accepting the 2 free books and gifts places me under no obligation to buy anything. I can always return a shipment and cancel at any time. Even if I never buy another book, the two free books and gifts are mine to keep forever.

225/326 HDN FVP7

Name _____ (PLEASE PRINT)

Address _____ Apt. #

City _____ State/Prov. _____ Zip/Postal Code

Signature (if under 18, a parent or guardian must sign)

Mail to the **Harlequin® Reader Service:**
IN U.S.A.: P.O. Box 1867, Buffalo, NY 14240-1867
IN CANADA: P.O. Box 609, Fort Erie, Ontario L2A 5X3

Want to try two free books from another line?
Call 1-800-873-8635 or visit www.ReaderService.com.

* Terms and prices subject to change without notice. Prices do not include applicable taxes. Sales tax applicable in N.Y. Canadian residents will be charged applicable taxes. Offer not valid in Quebec. This offer is limited to one order per household. Not valid for current subscribers to Harlequin Desire books. All orders subject to credit approval. Credit or debit balances in a customer's account(s) may be offset by any other outstanding balance owed by or to the customer. Please allow 4 to 6 weeks for delivery. Offer available while quantities last.

Your Privacy—The Harlequin® Reader Service is committed to protecting your privacy. Our Privacy Policy is available online at www.ReaderService.com or upon request from the Harlequin Reader Service.

We make a portion of our mailing list available to reputable third parties that offer products we believe may interest you. If you prefer that we not exchange your name with third parties, or if you wish to clarify or modify your communication preferences, please visit us at www.ReaderService.com/consumerchoice or write to us at Harlequin Reader Service Preference Service, P.O. Box 9062, Buffalo, NY 14269. Include your complete name and address.

HDI3

**SPECIAL EXCERPT FROM
HARLEQUIN® DESIRE**

USA TODAY Bestselling Author

Catherine Mann

presents

PLAYING FOR KEEPS

Available April 2013 from Harlequin® Desire!

Midway through the junior high choir's rehearsal of "It's a Small World," Celia Patel found out just how small the world could shrink.

She dodged as half the singers—the female half—sprinted down the stands, squealing in fan-girl glee. All their preteen energy was focused on racing to where he stood.

Malcolm Douglas.

Seven-time Grammy Award winner.

Platinum-selling soft rock star.

And the man who'd broken Celia's heart when they were both sixteen years old.

Malcolm raised a stalling hand to his ominous bodyguards while keeping his eyes locked on Celia, smiling that million-watt grin. Tall and honed, he still had a hometown-boy-handsome appeal. He'd merely matured—now polished with confidence and whipcord muscle.

She wanted him gone.

For her sanity's sake, she *needed* him gone. But now that he was here, she couldn't look away.

He wore his khakis and Ferragamo loafers with the easy confidence of a man comfortable in his skin. Sleeves rolled up on his chambray shirt exposed strong, tanned forearms and musician's hands.

Best not to think about his talented, nimble hands.

His sandy-brown hair was as thick as she remembered. It was still a little long, skimming over his forehead in a way that once called to her fingers to stroke it back. And those blue eyes—heaven help her…

There was no denying, he was all man now.

What in the hell was he doing here?

Malcolm hadn't set foot in Azalea, Mississippi, since a judge crony of her father's had offered Malcolm the choice of juvie or military reform school nearly eighteen years ago. Since he'd left her behind—scared, *pregnant* and determined to salvage her life.

But they weren't sixteen anymore, and she'd put aside reckless dreams the day she'd handed her newborn daughter over to a couple who could give the precious child everything Celia and Malcolm couldn't.

She threw back her shoulders and started across the gym.

She refused to let Malcolm's appearance yank the rug out from under her blessedly routine existence. She refused to give him the power to send her pulse racing.

She refused to let Malcolm Douglas threaten the future she'd built for herself.

What is Malcolm doing back in town?

Find out in

PLAYING FOR KEEPS

Available April 2013 from Harlequin® Desire!

HARLEQUIN *Desire*

ALWAYS POWERFUL, PASSIONATE AND PROVOCATIVE.

When fashionista Lily Zaccaro goes undercover to find out who's stealing her company's secrets, she can't resist sleeping with the enemy, her new British billionaire boss, Nigel Statham.

Look for
PROJECT: RUNAWAY HEIRESS

by Heidi Betts

part of the
Project: Passion miniseries!

Available April 2013 from Harlequin Desire wherever books are sold.

Project: Passion
On the runway, in the bedroom, down the aisle—these high-flying fashionistas mean business.

Powerful heroes…scandalous secrets…burning desires.

HD73238

HARLEQUIN® *Desire*

ALWAYS POWERFUL, PASSIONATE AND PROVOCATIVE.

The last thing Robert Caroselli needs is
marketing hotshot Carolyn Taylor telling him
how to run the family business…and for her to
be pregnant with his child! Sure, he'll inherit
millions for becoming a proud papa….but is
becoming a loving husband part of the bargain?

Look for

CAROSELLI'S BABY CHASE

by Michelle Celmer, part of
The Caroselli Inheritance miniseries!

*Available April 2013 from Harlequin Desire
wherever books are sold!*

The Caroselli Inheritance:
Ten million dollars to produce an heir.
The clock is ticking.

Also available in the series:
CAROSELLI'S CHRISTMAS BABY
November 2012

Powerful heroes…scandalous secrets…burning desires.